I saw the glint of something metal
in the glare of the overhead light
and realized a moment later
that it was a small crowbar.

"Hey," I said, but the word was lost in the pelting rain. The person next to the truck reached up and smashed the passenger window of the red pickup truck.

"Hey!" I said it louder the second time. I was on the move, baseball bat clenched firmly in my right hand, and this time the sound of my voice got through.

I was mad, and when I get mad I don't always stop to think ahead.

I headed for the fence without considering the alternatives. When something hit me hard on the back of the head, the only reaction I had time for was a kind of dazed surprise.

I remember one moment of standing there in the rain, realizing I'd been hit, listening to the wind and the dripping of water off the roof.

And then I got suddenly very dizzy, and everything went away.

Dear Reader,

Happy Holidays, 1993, and welcome to the Literacy Volunteers of Orange-Athol inaugural novel by Cathy Stanton. Cathy writes as Cathryn Clare for Silhouette Books, New York. An Athol resident, she conceived this very appropriate fund-raising plan as a salute both to fun and literacy while honoring generous businesses and individuals in the North Quabbin area.

In order to serve businesses and individuals well in this fictional work, Cathy found it necessary to limit the number included. The good news is she plans future holiday novels so others will have a chance to be part of the action.

Cathy's interest in Literacy Volunteers has extended naturally from her long-time service to the organization as tutor and coordinator. She has seen LVOA through expansion and transformation. Tutors, students, and board representatives have appreciated her sensitive, talented leadership.

After years of service to LVOA, Cathy has decided to devote herself full time to writing. *Trouble In Tow* is ample evidence that she has earned the right to pursue her star.

As Cathy's publication list reveals, she is a writer of varied talents and interests with nine Silhouette novels to her credit. She is also a playwright and has contributed to a range of periodical publications.

LVOA will miss Cathy's daily attention but looks forward to her continuing involvement as tutor and volunteer.

Oh, yes. And, as she has promised, *Trouble In Tow* is just the first of a series. So, just wait till next year.

Board of Directors
Literacy Volunteers of Orange-Athol

CATHY STANTON
TROUBLE IN TOW

**LITERACY VOLUNTEERS
OF ORANGE-ATHOL**

PUBLISHED BY HALEY'S
ATHOL, MASSACHUSETTS

LITERACY VOLUNTEERS
OF ORANGE-ATHOL
in cooperation with HALEY'S
Post Office Box 248
Athol, MA   01331

TROUBLE IN TOW

International Standard Book Number: 0-9626308-2-9
Library of Congress Catalogue Number: 93-080125

First Edition. First Printing. November 1993.

Imagemaking by the *Athol Daily News.*
Book design by Mary Pat Spaulding and Marcia Gagliardi.
Cover photography by Robert Mayer.
Caricatures by Ann Reed.
Copy read by Marcia Gagliardi. Proof read by Ellen Hargis.
Layout formatted in Aldus Pagemaker 5.0.
Printed by the Highland Press.

Also by Cathy Stanton

Romantic Suspense Novels
written using the pseudonym *Cathryn Clare*
for *Silhouette Intimate Moments*
Sweet Shadows, publication date to be announced
Sun and Shadow, to be released in March 1994
Chasing Destiny, June 1993

Romance Novels
written using the pseudonym *Cathryn Clare*
for *Silhouette Desire*
Hot Stuff, January, 1992
The Midas Touch, September 1991
Five by Ten, September 1990
Lock, Stock and Barrel, September 1990
Blind Justice, July 1989
To the Highest Bidder, January 1988

Short Mystery Fiction
*Multiple Submissions, **Alfred Hitchcock's Mystery Magazine,***
September 1989
*The Teddy Bears' Wake, **Alfred Hitchcock's Mystery Magazine,***
August 1988

CATHY STANTON

was born in Canada in 1958. She worked for several years in Toronto as a flutist, singer, and storyteller. She was an arts administrator before moving to the Boston area in 1983. She and her husband Fred Holmgren, a classical trumpet player, have lived in Athol since 1988, and Cathy has been a full-time writer since then. Her novels have been translated into ten languages and have sold more than a million copies worldwide.

She has also pursued an interest in theatre. Her plays have been staged in Toronto and at Gettysburg College, Pennsylvania, and given readings in Boston and New York.

A member of the Dramatists Guild, Sisters in Crime, and Romance Writers of America, Cathy has also been actively involved in Literacy Volunteers of America since 1988. As part of an interdisciplinary program at Vermont College, Montpelier, she is pursuing a degree in history.

She is aided in all her writing endeavors by "the view of the forest out my window and three helpful cats."

This book is dedicated to everyone
who made it possible—
and especially to Marcia,
who also made it fun.

PROLOGUE

"I don't know, Rita." My banker looked doubtful. "The figure for the new truck is pretty steep."

"I've got to have something newer," I said. I had rehearsed this scene in my mind over and over, and I was determined to sound poised, professional, and not as if I was begging. The truth was, though, I was pretty close to desperate, and the banker and I both knew it.

"And I've got to have somebody to drive for me, at least part-time," I said. "I've been managing on my own, but you know this is a hard business to survive in unless you can compete. And I can't compete unless I expand. It's as simple as that."

"Hmm." I'd been banking at North Quabbin Savings and Loan for years, and they've always been good to me. And maybe it was just my imagination that was painting the prospective picture so bleak, but at that moment, I could almost see into my banker's head, where all those bankerly terms like collateral and credit risk and depreciation were not balancing in my favor.

He didn't say anything else, just that he would take some time to go over what I'd given him and have an answer for me next Monday. It was Thursday now, and the prospect of a weekend wondering whether I was going to survive in the towing business didn't appeal to me.

But there didn't seem to be any way around it. I needed the money, and badly, and I was just going to have to trust to the good judgment of the North Quabbin Savings and Loan and hope that the weekend was busy enough to take my mind off the fact that my future was hanging in the balance.

I got my wish. The weekend was as unlikely as anything I could have dreamed up, and when it was over, several things about my life were not quite the same.

1

ONE

It started with the proverbial dark and stormy night.

Dark and stormy nights are my bread and butter. I do a lot of my work when the weather's bad, when the roads ice up and people's windshield wipers can't keep pace with the rain. It's not that I'm personally pleased when a lot of cars are going off the road, but it is good for the towing business.

I run a company called Henry's Towing, although my name isn't Henry. It's Rita—Rita Magritte. Henry was my husband, but he died eight years ago. He was the driver, I was the dispatcher and bookkeeper, and after he died I couldn't imagine giving it up.

To be honest, I couldn't *afford* to give it up. All we really had in the way of assets were an aging wrecker and a modest local reputation for being reliable and friendly, no matter what the circumstances. We never thought Henry would die suddenly at forty-nine, or that I would be left a forty-year-old widow with two teen-aged kids and no particular marketable skills outside the towing business.

So I stuck with it. I learned to drive the truck, and to hook things up to it, and I'd been running the company by myself for eight years now. My kids told me I was nuts, but kids always think their parents are nuts. Just lately I had been finding it too hard to make ends meet on my own, though. I had spent a lot of time going over the books, after a long day of work, and the books had been telling me some unmistakable things. Henry's Towing had always been a modest little business, but recently I had been losing out to bigger, better-equipped companies, and if I wanted to stand a chance of keeping things going, I knew I was going to have to build Henry's up, and soon.

The only way I could afford to do that was to take out a bank loan. I wished my banker hadn't looked at me with the same expression as my kids did when I told them I was going to take over the company in the first place, but it was too late to do anything but cross my fingers now.

So I was grateful for the dark and stormy night. When the weather turns ugly, I don't have time to let things weigh on my

3

mind. Then, I mostly just try to keep ahead of the calls that come in.

Two came in at once on that particular Thursday evening. It was an awful night, gusty and raw with the rain coming down in sheets, the kind of late-October rain that knocks the pretty colors right off the trees and lets you know another New England winter is on its merry way. I had just come in from hauling somebody's motor home out of a soggy field in New Salem, and I was kind of hoping to get a few minutes to grab a cup of coffee and maybe a sandwich. But the phone was ringing as I stood in my hallway shaking the water off my raincoat, and I had no sooner taken the call—for a car in a pond on Route 78 near the New Hampshire border—than the phone rang again. It was shaping up to be a busy night.

The second call was somebody whose pickup truck had skidded off a road up in North Orange. I'm based in Orange, and there are a lot of miles of empty countryside between me and where the guy was calling from. He sounded about twenty years old and shaken up. "I really need to use it this evening," he kept saying. "And I think maybe the frame is bent."

"I'll get it back on the road," I told him, "but you're not going anywhere this evening if the frame's bent."

"Oh, man." I heard him conferring with someone near him, a young woman, I thought. There was anxiety in her voice, too. "Maybe it'll still drive," he said. I couldn't tell which of us he was speaking to. "Oh, *man*. Of all the nights for this to happen..." Something in his voice sounded badly disappointed, as though he'd just lost something precious that he couldn't possibly afford to replace.

"Look," I said, "I've got another call up on Route 78. But you're on my way to get to it. Why don't I pull you out and see whether your truck runs? If it does, you can pay me and be on your way. If it doesn't, I'll come back and tow it after I get done with my other call."

"Oh, man..." I heard indecision in his voice. "What are we going to do if it doesn't run?"

"Hey, I'm sorry, but that's not my problem." I'd said the phrase many times before. Tow truck drivers meet a lot of unhappy people. In my eight years of driving, I've learned how to sound sympathetic without actually encouraging people to confide in me further. I have a hard enough time making ends meet; if I started offering a shoulder to cry on, too, I'd be out of business in no time.

As it was, I might be out of business soon anyway. And that was what got me into this whole crazy business: I could hear in the kid's voice the same kind of urgency I'd been feeling myself lately, the same sense of *What am I going to do if this doesn't work?* It made me curious, and it ended up getting me involved in spite of myself.

"All right." The kid said the words quickly, like he'd just made up his mind. "Maybe it'll be okay." He gave a short laugh that didn't sound happy. "It's got to be okay," he said. "I don't know what we're going to do if it's not."

I wrote down his description of where his truck was, made a couple of empathetic comments about small winding roads on rainy nights, and said I'd be there as soon as I could.

My truck was one Henry had bought the year before he died. It was going on nine years old, which is ancient for a tow truck. Lately, things had been going wrong with it; it needed a starter motor, and there was a lot of rust. My son Mike is a mechanic, and he was doing what he could to keep the old beast on the road, but lately he had taken to shaking his head at it like a doctor who's not quite ready to break the news of a terminal illness.

I felt bad making the old wrecker do all the work, but the truth was that I couldn't afford to turn down a single tow call, especially if I was going to qualify for any kind of loan. I needed to grab all the work I could get, and that meant putting the tow truck on the road no matter what the weather.

It's too bad hindsight isn't something you can take to the bank. If I'd known then what I was getting into, I probably would have had my calls rerouted, locked the place up for the night, and just climbed into bed with a hot cup of tea.

I nearly missed the pickup the first time. It wasn't hard to see why the kid had driven off the road: there was a jaw-breaking bump in just the wrong place, and if you swerved to miss it, you ended up negotiating with a fast-moving stream of water cutting across the pavement right at a sudden turn. Probably a culvert backed up, I thought. We'd had a lot of rain lately, and the stream across the road was nearly big enough to qualify for inclusion on the map.

I slowed down to get past all these hazards and only noticed the truck because my headlights caught a faint gleam off its rear bumper. I frowned. Usually, when people called a tow truck, I found them waiting eagerly by the side of the road, or at least hopping out of the front seat when they saw my headlights. The red pickup truck was so far off the pavement that I couldn't be sure, but at a cursory glance it seemed to be empty.

"Well, hell," I said. I pulled over to the side of the road and got out my flashlight. I left the truck engine running, and it made a familiar sound in the middle of thrashing tree branches and the pelting of the rain against the road, the windshield, against everything.

The pickup truck *was* empty. And it was locked. I couldn't see anything in the cab except a take-out container and two soda cans. The truck had sunk into the soft ground on its passenger side, and there was a big rock between it and the road, which might explain the driver's fears that he'd bent the frame.

I looked around. The woods are unnerving at night, and it makes them even creepier when you shine a light into them. It isn't anything you can see, it's the feeling that somewhere, just out of the light, things are watching you. I grew up in Athol, which is a small place, but at least it's a town. I never got used to being in the middle of a lot of trees at night, especially with the wind blowing and the branches making swooping motions as though they were aiming at you.

I was even less happy that my potential customer wasn't around. I remembered passing a lighted house not far back on the road and decided to take a chance on the kids being there. Most people, when they're stranded, will hike back to the last place they passed.

This is the part I wouldn't have done if I'd had the benefit of hindsight. I kept thinking of that young man's tone of voice on the phone; he'd sounded as though someone had told him his birthday might not come this year, after all, and he might not get the party he'd been promised. I was about to ignore my own very sensible rules about not letting sympathy interfere with business, and you'll see where it landed me.

I turned the tow truck around with difficulty and maneuvered into the driveway of the lighted house. The man who answered the door—a young guy with a beard—looked surprised.

"Yeah, they were here," he said, in answer to my question about two wet strangers with a story about a pickup truck. "Young guy, and his girlfriend. Seemed pretty upset. They called from here."

"So," I said, as pleasantly as I could, "where are they now?"

That was what he'd been looking surprised about, he told me. "They said they were going to go wait in the cab of the truck. Are you sure they aren't there?"

I said I was sure. "Did they say anything else?" I asked.

"They said something about this ruining everything. Like they had big plans and they needed wheels to get to them. Oh, and they made one other call."

"Who to?"

"I wasn't listening." He sounded slightly offended. "The guy did sound happier after he'd hung up."

"Well, hell," I said again, more emphatically this time. The bearded guy looked startled. I've been told I have a grandmotherly aura, which, at forty-eight, I don't always choose to take as a compliment. But I know that my appearance—a broad, fairly ordinary face, permed auburn hair, and a figure that my friends call 'ample' when they're trying to think of something nice to say about my shape—all of that leads people to think of me as far more matronly than I really am.

The great thing about being forty-eight is that I've gotten past caring what people think of me. I thanked the neighbor for his help, and hiked back out into the rain.

It hadn't eased up any. In fact, the weather seemed to be working itself into the kind of storm that could mean all kinds of accidents before the night was through. I was going to have to decide what to do about the abandoned truck, and soon.

The thing was, it annoyed me to have wasted even this much time and to have nothing to show for it. And—I have to admit this, because I know it's what got me in trouble—I was a little bit concerned about the missing young man and his girlfriend. I couldn't forget the frightening blackness of the woods all around their truck, and it wasn't a night to be out hiking. If they weren't at the house and they weren't in the truck, then where were they?

I called myself any number of names while I was doing it, but that didn't stop me from driving on up the road to see whether there might be another house up there. There was, just a half-mile farther on. There were lights on inside, and I put the hood of my raincoat up and hurried to the front door, hoping that my missing couple would have taken shelter inside and this would be the end of my crazy quest.

It wasn't. It just got more mystifying. A neat, gray-haired man of about seventy answered my knock, with an expectant look on his face that vanished when he saw me.

"Good heavens," he said. "Who are you?"

"Rita Magritte, Henry's Towing." I explained what had happened.

"Good heavens," the man said again. "That must be the young couple I was expecting."

"They were coming to see you?"

"Yes. To have a picture appraised."

I hadn't seen a picture in the truck, but then, I hadn't been able to get a good look behind the seat. I looked more closely at the elderly man. "What was the guy's name?" I asked.

"Tom. That's all I know. He and his girlfriend had just bought a local landscape in someone's antique shop, and Tom had an idea it might be valuable. He described it to me on the phone, and I agreed it was worth taking a look at. That's literally the extent of what I know about it, Miss—uh, Mrs. Magritte."

"He didn't call you after his truck slid off the road?"

"No. In fact, when I heard you at the door, I assumed it was Tom. That's why I was so surprised to see you instead."

"Are you an antique dealer?"

"In a modest way." He reached for a small table next to the door, and pulled a business card out of a brass bowl. *McGarrity Brooks*, it read. *Antique Tools and Ephemera*.

"What's 'ephemera?'" I asked.

"In my case, it means the odd appraisal, the occasional publication, odds and ends to flesh out a schoolteacher's pension." McGarrity Brooks was beginning to look concerned now. "Look here, Mrs. Magritte, what do you suppose happened to those young people? It's hardly a night to be out walking."

"I know."

"And you're sure they're not with the truck?"

"Quite sure." I pulled the hood of my raincoat back over my head. "Well, sorry to bother you, Mr. Brooks. I'd better be getting back to work."

"I wonder if I should call the police." He seemed quite flustered now. I looked around his living room; it was full of knick-knacks and old tools and little display cases, all neatly arranged and more dust-free than my house has been in the past eight years. I could picture McGarrity Brooks fussing over anything that went wrong, from a misplaced book on a shelf to a missing customer on a wet night.

"I'll let them know what's going on," I said. "Thanks for your help."

The rain hadn't let up any. In fact, it seemed fiercer than ever as I wasted another ten minutes driving up and then down the isolated road again, just in case there was a young couple out in the rain.

If they were there, they were well-hidden. I drove back to the pickup truck, telling myself this was all the time I was going to spend on this wild-goose chase. I got my flashlight out again, and peered into the cab, thinking maybe they'd left a note that I hadn't seen the first time.

There was no note. There were just the empty fast-food container, the two soda bottles, and the howling, lashing forest all around me. "That does it," I said out loud, and immediately wished I hadn't spoken. Saying something out loud implies, after all, that there's someone there to hear you, and I didn't like that idea much.

So I kept the rest of my thoughts to myself as I climbed back into the tow truck and headed for Route 78. When I got there, I found out that my search for Tom and his girlfriend had cost me my other job: another tow truck was just pulling away, with the customer that should have been mine.

I pounded the dashboard in a very ungrandmotherly way, and said some things I was glad no one was around to hear. This kid, whoever he was, had called me out and then vanished, and worse yet, he'd gotten me interested enough in his disappearance that I'd spent time on him that had cost me a paying customer. Instead of two fees, I was left with none, and that made me mad.

When I get mad, I don't sit and stew about it. My husband Henry used to do that, and it drove me crazy. My way is to take some action, do something that makes me feel better, and then put the whole problem behind me.

In this case, I had the remedy right at hand. The driver of the red pickup truck might have disappeared, but he had, after all, called me out to tow his vehicle. And so I did tow it, all the way back to my yard on Airport Road in Orange, where I locked it securely inside the chain-link fence. I decided it could just sit there until its owner showed up and recompensed me for my time and trouble. On a night like tonight, I couldn't afford to be working for free.

It didn't put any money in my pocket, but it did make me feel a little better as I grabbed a quick sandwich and headed out for my next call. The wild night kept me as busy as I'd guessed it would, and it was nearly two-thirty by the time I got to bed.

When I finally did, I was almost too tired to give my usual good-night wave at my husband's picture on the wall. Our son and daughter had paid to have Henry's caricature done by a local artist, Ann Reed, at a fair ten years ago. It was still my favorite picture of him. Ann had captured the glint in his eye perfectly and the little grin that meant he probably had something up his sleeve, too.

HENRY MAGRITTE

I had gotten into the habit of telling the picture good-night not long after Henry died, and I'd never gotten back out of it again. Tonight, though, I barely took the time to mutter "'Night, Henry" as I went down the hall and into the bedroom. I was asleep as soon as my head hit the pillow and would have slept like a baby for hours if my dog hadn't started barking at four A.M.

TWO

The dog's name is Chili. I got him after Henry died, partly for protection, partly for companionship, partly because I've always liked big black mutts with little brown eyebrows. Chili Dog is eight years old, but he doesn't know that. He still carries on like a puppy, especially when there's a stranger on the property. It's his most marketable skill, and he was employing it now.

I could hear him even over the wind, which was still howling. "This better be something more interesting than a raccoon, Chili," I muttered, as I forced my eyelids open and pulled on a pair of pants under my flannel nightgown. My raincoat was still damp when I shrugged into it at the back door.

I didn't turn any lights on. There was one big overhead light on the lot, and it was bright enough to see by. At first everything looked normal, except for Chili Dog bounding and straining at the end of his leash, but then something moved.

It looked like a shadow, crouched over, slipping between the rows of vehicles. There were half a dozen cars and trucks in there tonight, vehicles I'd towed in that were now waiting for their owners to arrange for them to be moved somewhere else, or to pay the tow fees. Nobody is supposed to be inside the chain-link fence except me and the dog. The silent, shadowy figure I could see in there now meant that somebody was up to no good.

I slipped back inside the house and called the police. The Orange police station was right down the road, but thanks to some budget cuts a couple of years ago, the Orange police no longer worked an all-night shift. I had to call the state police, who were several miles away in Athol.

A security system was one of the many improvements I was hoping to make if I got the loan I had applied for. I had all kinds of laudable plans: get my signs repainted, join the North Quabbin Chamber of Commerce, call my friend at Whittier Heating about adding some heat to my garage, maybe get some hats made up with "Henry's Towing" on them. None of that did me any good at the moment.

And at the moment, security still consisted of Chili Dog and an old baseball bat I kept by the back door for emergencies. If somebody managed to make away with one of the vehicles on my lot before the state police showed up, that would qualify as an emergency, so I picked up the bat and went back outside as quietly as I could. It was hardly high-tech, but if this was just some kid trying to rip off an unattended car, I hoped it would look threatening enough to do the trick.

I couldn't tell, from the size of the moving shadow, whether it was a kid or an adult, male or female. Whoever it was had slipped along one row of cars and stopped next to the truck I'd pulled in from the ditch in North Orange, the one whose driver had disappeared. Chili Dog was beside himself, trying to get loose, and his barking was starting to sound hoarse and hysterical. I wanted to murmur to him to calm down, that things were under control, but I didn't want to let my intruder know I was there until I had a better idea what was up.

I found out in a hurry. I saw the glint of something metal in the glare of the overhead light, and realized a moment later that it was a small crowbar. "Hey," I said, but the word was lost in the pelting rain and the sudden tinkle of breaking glass as the person next to the truck reached up and smashed the passenger window of the red pickup truck.

"Hey!" I said it louder the second time. I was on the move, baseball bat clenched firmly in my right hand, and this time the sound of my voice got through. The shadow shifted suddenly and darted away down the row of vehicles.

I guess I automatically assumed that he—or she—was retreating, probably the way they'd come. I could see the hole that had been cut in the chain-link fence now, at the back corner of the lot. I hurried in that direction, trying to cut off the escape route I was sure the interloper would be taking.

I was mad—mad that anybody would cut through my fence and vandalize a vehicle on my property, mad that I had had to get up and go out in the driving rain yet again tonight—and as I've already said, when I get mad I don't always stop to think ahead. It didn't occur to me that the stranger might be setting a trap for me instead of high-tailing it out of there.

So I headed for the fence without considering the alternatives, and when something hit me hard on the back of the head, the only reaction I had time for was a kind of dazed surprise. I remember one moment—astonishingly clear in my memory, even now—of standing there in the rain, realizing I'd been hit, listening to the wind and the dripping of water off the roof of the house and Chili Dog just about to lose his voice. And then I got suddenly very dizzy, and everything went away.

"People have been known to drown in puddles."

The words made no sense to me at first. I was lying in bed, having the strangest dream, and for some reason I couldn't get my eyes open. At least the dog had stopped barking, I thought. Now, if I could just figure out the remark about puddles...

"She's lucky she didn't land face down."

Another voice joined in. "Or that whoever hit her wasn't trying any harder to crack her skull."

I frowned, and realized that the reason I couldn't open my eyes was that it hurt too much even to think about it. I wondered who the voices were, and where I was.

"She has a hard head." This was a third voice, a woman, sounding slightly amused. "I went to school with her. She used to get hit with softballs and never complain."

I knew that voice, but trying to identify it made my whole head throb. I was waking up now, and coming to the unpleasant realization that everything from my neck up ached, and the more I woke up, the worse it got.

"She'll be complaining about this," the first voice said. "She's got a nasty lump already. Good thing it didn't break the surface."

Something touched the back of my head, something that in retrospect was probably feather-light. It didn't feel light at the time; it felt as though somebody had just slugged me with the baseball bat I'd been holding when I'd been knocked unconscious.

"Ow," I said, as loudly as I could. Bells went off in my head from the effort of getting the single syllable out.

"Ow, yourself." I felt a sympathetic hand squeeze mine. It was the third voice speaking, the one I knew but couldn't quite place. "I bet you're wishing you'd stayed asleep a while longer."

I gave the tiniest of nods. The bell-ringing got louder.

"Just lie quietly," the voice said. "I called Hannah, and she's coming over."

"Where am I?" Maybe I just mouthed the words, I don't know. But my question seemed to get through.

"You're at the hospital, Rita. In the emergency room. You got a nasty knock on the head. The police found you, and called an ambulance. Why don't you take it easy until Hannah gets here?"

Hannah is my daughter. She's twenty-four, newly-married, and far more of a respectable matron than I'll ever be. Getting a call from the hospital emergency room that her mother had been knocked out by a crowbar-wielding intruder would have thrown her into an absolute fit by now, I thought. It didn't make my headache any easier to take.

It did wake me up some, though, at least enough to recognize the friendly voice. "Belle?" I said, and the hand holding mine squeezed again, warmly.

"You're going to be all right," she said, as though my being able to identify my old school friend Belle Fountaine confirmed that fact. "I've been telling everybody in ER that you're finally old enough and wise enough to lie still when you're told to, so don't go proving me wrong, okay?"

Things hurt badly enough that for a little while there wasn't much chance of proving her wrong. But in spite of my monster headache, I couldn't stop thinking. I found myself wanting desperately to know what had happened after I'd been knocked out and before the police arrived. Was the red pickup truck still on my parking lot? What had someone been looking for, and why was it so important that it was worth knocking me out to get it?

I finally managed to get my eyes open, in search of somebody to provide me with some answers. The light was painfully bright, but after squinting for a few minutes, I started to recognize my surroundings, and to feel less disoriented than I had been.

I'd spent time in the emergency room of Athol Memorial Hospital before this, but I'd always been in the waiting room, waiting for a child to be repaired—usually my son Mike, usually after a bicycle or sports-related mishap. The last time I'd been here had been the awful night Henry had had his heart attack, and I'd sat by myself for the longest half hour of my life until someone had come out and told me he hadn't made it. Belle hadn't been working in the ER then, but a nurse equally concerned and kindhearted had stayed with me until I'd absorbed the worst of the shock. I can't say being there brought back a lot of happy memories, but I knew that I was in the capable hands of people who cared what happened to me.

That made me feel a little bit guilty as I countermanded Belle's instructions by struggling to a sitting position and preparing to slide off the bed where I'd been lying. The room swayed as I did it, and the nurse who had stayed with me protested, but I kept moving, although it was slow, and finally got to my feet.

Nobody looked impressed by that as I winced my way out to the reception area. Hannah was there, neatly dressed—even as a small child, she refused to go out on the street until she'd combed her hair and re-tied her shoelaces at least twice—and she and the receptionist and Belle were having a heart-to-heart. I was pretty sure it was about me, because I caught the phrase "Make sure she rests" and saw a budding look of disapproval on Hannah's face.

Hannah is a good person, but she's never quite gotten over the fact that her mother drives a tow truck instead of behaving like a sedate middle-aged widow. She rolled her eyes at me as I tottered into the hall, and Belle said, "Oh, Rita, honestly."

"Don't yell at me," I said. "I'm in enough pain as it is."

"At least sit down," Hannah said. "You look *terrible*, Mom."

"Thanks," I said. "If I sit down, I'm just going to have to get up again at some point. Do I have to stay, Belle, or can I get Hannah to take me home to my own bed?"

Belle consulted with the ER doctor, both of them looking just as disapproving as Hannah. Disapproval or not, though, it seemed they didn't have any urgent medical reason to keep me. They did insist on taking some X-rays, which apparently showed that my head wasn't cracked anywhere, and they were lobbying to keep me for a CAT scan, but by then—it was nine A.M.—I had announced I was going home.

Hannah started to lay down the law to me in her car on the way there. "This is absolutely it, Mom," she said. "You can't keep running the towing business by yourself. What if that guy had had a gun or something?"

"Was it a guy?" I let her reproaches roll off me, and concentrated on what I was most interested in knowing.

"I mean, you can't go on relying on that dog to protect you against—" She finally paused long enough to realize I'd spoken. "What do you mean, was it a guy?" she asked me.

"Whoever broke in. Did they catch him? Do they know it was a man?"

"I don't have any idea. All I know is I got a phone call two minutes before I was on my way to work, telling me my mother had been found unconscious in her own yard. Beyond that, I don't know anything. And if you know anything, I hope to heaven you'll let the police know, and let them handle it, because—"

I'd been right about the fits. Hannah insisted on stopping at Bruce's Pharmacy to fill the prescription the hospital had given me, and then she harangued me all the way to my house. I closed my eyes and decided it didn't really matter to me whether she thought I was listening or sleeping. When we got home, I thanked her sincerely for coming and getting me, and said I hoped she wouldn't get chewed out for being late to work. She works at the Worker's Credit Union, on the other side of Orange.

"If you think I have any intention of leaving you alone in this house," she began, but I didn't let her finish this time.

"I'll be fine," I said. "Whatever the person was after, they've got it by now." I could see, now that we were in the driveway, that the red pickup was still there. The passenger window was a gaping hole surrounded by shards of safety glass, and the lingering drizzle in the morning air was no doubt finding its way into the cab.

18

"At least promise me you'll call the police to tell them you're home," Hannah said.

It was easy to make the promise, because I wanted to find out what the police knew, anyway. I listened to Hannah's remaining objections, let her feed Chili Dog his breakfast because she was desperate to make herself useful, and finally shooed her off to work, after practically swearing on the family Bible that I wouldn't consider taking any towing calls today.

It wasn't hard to promise that, either. I still felt light-headed, although I suspected only part of it was from the bump on my skull. I'd had less than two hours of sleep before the dog had wakened me, and I knew I had to do something about that before I did anything else. I changed into my spare pajamas—I was still wearing my work pants and flannel nightgown, and they'd gotten pretty grubby during the night's adventures—and crawled into bed after calling my answering service to ask them to re-route my calls to Jim's Auto. I needed a few hours' sleep before heading back into the daylight to see if I could find out who had hit me over the head and broken into the mysterious red pickup truck.

THREE

"Tom Wilson." The state police officer put her finger on the page in front of her. "That's the name of the guy who owns the truck you towed. And you say you haven't heard from him since that first phone call?"

"Not a word." I put my hand up to the back of my head, cautiously exploring the lump my nighttime visitor had raised with the crowbar. "Unless he was the one who did this," I added. "What can you tell me about Mr. Tom Wilson?"

I knew the state cop slightly. She was new, but we'd already crossed paths at the scenes of a couple of accidents. My slight acquaintance, though, wasn't enough to get me an answer to my question. "Come on, Rita," she said. "You know I can't go opening people's files to you, just because you ask."

"I *did* get hit on the head," I pointed out. "And Tom Wilson's vehicle is still on my lot. If he was the one who was there last night, trying to get his truck back, he may try again. Doesn't that give me the right to a little information about him?"

She shook her head. "Let the police handle this," she said. "We'll be keeping an eye on your place until this gets sorted out, don't worry about that. But let us do the investigating, all right?"

"You sound like my daughter," I told her.

"Your daughter has good sense, then. Maybe you should listen to her."

I left the state police barracks in Athol feeling grumpy. I was driving the wrecker everywhere these days, because the frame on my car—an aging blue Toyota—had rusted out and I was trying to find a welder who would agree to stick it back together again for a price I could afford.

I still had a headache, and the determined drizzle in the air didn't improve my mood any. Neither did the stonewalling I'd just gotten. I knew the police couldn't share their information with any citizen who asked for it, but I had hoped I would be entitled to more than just a pat on my bruised head.

Well, at least I had a name. And I had time to track it down, since I'd asked Jim's Auto to cover my towing calls until tomorrow afternoon. The owner of Jim's was a friend of my husband Henry, and for old times' sake he helps me out when he can. He has always said he was happy to do it, although lately when I've had to call him, I've thought I detected overtones of "How long is Rita going to be able to keep that business going?" in his voice. I'd been wondering the same thing, although I didn't say that out loud. After Monday, when I knew about my loan, I would either be hiring myself some help or selling my equipment off to Jim's Auto or the highest bidder.

I didn't want to think about that today. My head hurt enough already, and there was nothing I could do until I called the North Quabbin Savings and Loan on Monday. So I went home and looked up Tom Wilson in the phone book.

There was only one T. Wilson listed in the immediate area. I called the number, and got no answer, which didn't surprise me. The red pickup truck I'd towed was fairly new, which spoke to me of an owner who was gainfully employed somewhere. My next question was, where?

Before I went out in search of an answer, I checked the pickup truck over thoroughly. The fast-food container was still in the front seat, and the two empty soda cans. The glove compartment had the usual odds and ends in it—maps, gas receipts, some little packets of plum sauce that suggested Tom had been eating Chinese recently. There was also a business card from Athol Travel, on Main Street in Athol. I pocketed the card, and then I got my flashlight and looked under the seat, where I found jumper cables, a tow cable, and a couple of crushed coffee cups.

There was no sign of the painting Tom had apparently been taking to have valued. If it had been there when I'd towed the truck in, it was gone now.

I got back in the tow truck and drove to Tom Wilson's address in Orange. He lived in a three-story house that had, judging by the number of electrical meters on the side, been divided up into four apartments.

The tow truck coughed a little when I turned off the ignition, and I patted the dashboard sympathetically. "Time for a tune-up, old girl," I said. "We'll see if Uncle Mike has time for you this evening, since we're off work anyway." The truck coughed again, as if to reassure me that I wasn't entirely nuts to be sitting here talking out loud to a vehicle, and then it finally settled down into silence.

No one answered when I rang the bell marked "T. Wilson." But I had seen a curtain twitch at one of the first-floor windows, so I rang the other bells until I got an answer. A young woman opened the front door, with a toddler hanging onto her knees.

No, she told me, Tom Wilson wasn't usually around during the day. She thought he got home from work around four-thirty. She frowned at the tow truck, parked at the curb.

"You're not here to re-possess his truck, are you?" she said, sounding concerned as well as curious. "He said he was finally almost clear on those old debts."

I smiled my friendliest, most grandmotherly smile, and said "No, of course not." Some tow companies handle re-possessions on the side, and Henry used to do a few, but I've never been able to bring myself to do it. Maybe the gender psychologists would say it's because I'm a woman, but I've always thought it was just because I'm always fairly close to insolvency myself. I tend to sympathize too much with the re-possessees.

"I'm just interested in talking to Tom, that's all," I went on. "Does he still work at Orange Oil?" I had followed an Orange Oil delivery truck from Airport Road, which is no doubt why the name popped into my head.

The young woman's gaze sharpened a little, as though she had caught something odd about my question but couldn't put her finger on what it was. "I didn't know he ever worked there," she said, more slowly. "He's been at that school supply place over in the Orange Industrial Park ever since I've known him."

I nodded as though I'd known that all along, but it had just slipped my mind. I thanked the woman and got back in the truck.

I didn't know all the businesses in the Orange Industrial Park, but it wasn't hard to find the one I wanted. Baker School Specialty was at the first crossroad, with a carved wooden sign identifying the big, low building set among tall pine trees. At the back of the warehouse next door, a big truck with "Baker!"

painted on its sides was being loaded, and the parking lot was full of cars, which led me to think that whatever Baker School Specialty made, they were thriving at it.

I found a parking space big enough for the wrecker, and waited while it went through its tubercular coughing routine again. It seemed to take longer every time I shut the engine off, and I hoped my son Mike would be able to work his usual magic on it tonight.

My luck with vehicles might be running low at the moment, but in the investigation department, I was on a roll. One of the women in the Baker office was a casual acquaintance of mine, someone I knew because she had a weekend dog-grooming business and occasionally worked on Chili when he got too ripe. She was obviously just finishing up lunch at her desk, and her eyes widened when she saw me.

"Hey, Rita Magritte," she said. "I was just reading about you in the paper."

A copy of the *Athol Daily News* was on the desk in front of her. The paper hits the stands just after noon, but my home-delivered copy doesn't arrive until later in the afternoon, and anyway, it hadn't occurred to me that my adventure of last night might be hot news.

Apparently it was. I looked over my friend's shoulder at the front-page item, and read the same facts I'd just gotten from the state police: someone had broken into my lot using a pair of heavy-duty wire-cutters; whoever it was gotten clean away; I had been knocked unconscious and a truck window had been broken; nothing had apparently been stolen; the police had arrived just minutes later and had seen no sign of the intruder; they were pursuing the possibility that the object of the break-in had been to steal a vehicle, or perhaps to re-claim one without paying the towing bill first.

"They even mentioned your dog," my friend said. "What a hero." She looked more carefully at me. I was wearing my usual working clothes, navy blue pants with a sweater to match and a jacket that said "Henry's Towing" on the back—nothing out of the ordinary, to the people who knew me. But I was still tired and sore, and it seemed to be showing. "Are you all right?" she asked me. "Getting hit with a crowbar—"

"I'm okay," I said. I don't like being fussed over. "Listen, I wonder if I could ask you something. It's related to what happened last night."

I had a feeling that normally she might have balked at being asked questions about a fellow employee, but getting hit on the head had made me kind of a folk hero, and I took advantage of it. My friend didn't know Tom Wilson, except as a name on a payroll ledger, but she offered to take me into the shop and see if we could find him. This detecting business wasn't so hard, I thought, especially when I was likely to stumble on acquaintances no matter where I went.

My dog-grooming friend turned me over to the foreman, a friendly guy who was in the middle of supervising some employees at the shrink-wrap tunnel. I watched as they fed small bulletin boards into the machine. I looked around me, and arrived at the conclusion that Baker School Specialty specialized in boards—bulletin boards and marker boards and chalk boards, and erasers to go with them. The shop was full of people assembling and packaging boards of all sizes, from lapboards to wall-sized combination units.

When the foreman had finished getting the shrink-wrap operation going to his satisfaction, he told me Tom Wilson had already gone for the weekend. "He and his girlfriend took today off," he said. "They had some vacation time coming to them, so they were taking Friday and Monday off."

"Does his girlfriend work here too?" I asked.

"Sure. Jeri Crozier."

"Tom and Jeri?" I know I sounded skeptical.

"Weird, huh? People kept making jokes about it, even before they started going out. In fact, that's how they first got together, because of the jokes."

The young guy who had been working with the foreman looked less pleased about the conversation. "Should be more like Amos and Andy," he muttered, and the foreman frowned at him.

"Tom's a nice kid," he said. "He works his tail off, takes all the overtime hours we offer him. You couldn't ask for a harder worker. Jeri's all right, too. She works the second shift now, so they don't see as much of each other. I don't blame them for wanting to go off by themselves for a weekend."

He shot another meaningful look at the employee who had spoken. I got the feeling there was something going on under the surface that I wasn't grasping, maybe because the noise in the shop was making my headache worse. I didn't get the point of the Amos and Andy reference, either, until later that night. "Do you happen to know where they were going this week-end?" I asked.

The foreman shook his head. "No idea," he said. "Wherever it was, they were pretty excited about it. Like they were going on a treasure hunt or something."

I remembered the impression I'd gotten from Tom Wilson on the phone last night, that his truck skidding off the road had ruined something he'd been looking forward to for a long time. What could it have been, I wondered, and was it possible he'd found another way to get to it, after all? Was that why he and his girlfriend had disappeared so completely into the night?

"I gotta go," the foreman was saying, while I stood there trying to think past the pounding in my forehead. "Anything else I can do for you?"

"No. Thanks for your help. No, wait a minute." I'd thought of one more question as the two of us had moved away from the shrink-wrap room. "Would you say Tom Wilson is the kind of guy who would use violence to get what he wanted?" The foreman didn't answer right away, so I prompted him. "Would he be capable of hitting somebody, do you think?" I asked.

He still seemed reluctant to answer, but finally he did. "Tom's cooled down a lot in the last couple of years," he said guardedly. "Meeting Jeri was good for him. Don't listen to Mr. Sour Grapes in there." He nodded at the other employee who'd muttered an unfriendly comment about Tom and Jeri. "He used to date Jeri, until Tom came along. You want my opinion, she's got a better deal now. Tom's not in some kind of trouble, is he?"

"I hope not." I was sincere about that, although the foreman's veiled remarks didn't inspire me with a lot of faith in the missing man. I might have a splitting headache, but I could still fill in the gaps between the lines: if Tom Wilson calmed down a lot, that presumably meant he'd once been pretty wild. Wild enough to hit someone over the head with a crowbar? I wondered. I wouldn't be able to guess about that until I found him.

FOUR

In spite of my headache, I was getting more and more determined to do that. But first I had a visit to pay, one I'd been putting off because I knew it was going to make me think about my financial situation, and that was something I was trying to put off until Monday.

I couldn't put off talking to my insurance agent, though. I needed to report last night's incident—although he probably already knew about it, if he'd looked at the *Daily News*—and to find out whether I was covered for the damage my mysterious visitor had done to Tom Wilson's truck and my chain-link fence.

Cornerstone Insurance has a bright storefront office on Main Street in Athol, and it felt good to step out of the rain and into its amiable atmosphere on this gray day. The woman at the desk behind the counter told me my agent was in and confirmed my guess that people in the office had already been discussing my exploits of last night.

"We're just glad to see you're still with us," she told me, and that reminded me of a fact that my headache had been obscuring for the last little while: that I was, in fact, lucky to be alive.

My agent commiserated with me about the headache and added, "I should have known it would take more than a crowbar to keep you out of commission."

"There seems," I said, thinking of my friend Belle, "to be a school of thought in this town that I have a pretty thick head."

"Well, we all know you have a determined one, at any rate." My agent was opening my file now, his face growing more serious. "As I recall, it took me a long time to convince you to add that extra coverage last year, to make sure you wouldn't be liable for any damage to vehicles on your lot."

"I finally said yes, didn't I?"

"Yes. So the policy covers you for the broken window."

Something in his voice made me think that wasn't the whole story. "And?" I prompted.

"Well, unfortunately you decided to increase your deductible at the same time. My guess is that for the amount of damage that was described in the paper, you'll probably end up paying out of pocket."

Increasing my deductible had seemed like such a sensible idea at the time. There had never been a break-in on our lot before, and I had been trying to economize any way I could. Now—although my agent was being too diplomatic to point it out—I realized I'd been penny wise and pound foolish. I was going to have to pay not only for the damage to Tom Wilson's car, but to get my fence repaired, too. For a moment my head pounded so hard I had to close my eyes.

"Hey, Rita, I didn't mean to upset you." My agent sounded concerned.

"It's all right," I said, opening my eyes again. It would have been comforting to blame the insurance company, but I knew this wasn't their fault. I didn't want to mention that unless I got my bank loan, I was going to have trouble coming up with the money I would need for the repairs. I didn't mention, either, that this only made me more determined to go after Tom Wilson if I could, to get at least his towing and storage charges out of him—and a few answers, too.

I drove by his apartment again, but there was still no answer when I rang the bell. I decided there wasn't much point in reconfirming something I already knew, which was that he was away for the weekend—maybe far away, if the business card from Athol Travel in his glove compartment was any indication.

Maybe I would have better luck at Jeri Crozier's place. There was a pay phone at the Shop 'n Save supermarket, and, I discovered, five Croziers listed locally. I pulled out all the change I had in my wallet, and decided to call them all until I found one where there was someone named Jeri in the family.

I got her on my third call. A male voice told me in unfriendly tones that Jeri was away. He didn't offer to take a message.

I didn't bother to leave one. I had an address now, from the listing in the phone book, and that was what I had really wanted. The pay phone at the Shop 'n Save was close to the deli, and the smell of food reminded me that I was hungry, and that there probably wasn't going to be time to cook a meal this evening. I took a number and stood in line, stomach rumbling, feeling grateful to whoever had decided to include barbecued chicken on the deli menu. I got a big foil bag of it to go, and got back into the wrecker.

The Crozier family lived in uptown Athol on a side street just past the small white building that housed the William Kessler Insurance Agency. Their house was big, but run-down. There were no curtains in most of the windows, and the awning over the back door had come loose from the house, so that a steady and depressing stream of water splashed onto the steps next to me when I knocked on the door. I heard barking inside, from at least two different dogs.

The thick set, dark haired man who finally opened the door looked as unwelcoming as the voice on the phone had sounded. I smiled pleasantly, and said I was looking for Jeri.

The man looked over my shoulder, to where I'd left the tow truck idling in the driveway. "What," he said, "you got a call here or something?"

"No." I maintained my smile. "I was looking for Jeri."

"Well, she's not home."

Another man, slightly younger than the first, had come into the kitchen now. They were both in their twenties, I guessed, both frowning at me, both drinking beer out of cans. The beer cans looked very comfortable in their hands, as though beer cans spent a lot of time there.

The second guy looked hard at me. "What's all this about Jeri all of a sudden?" he demanded. "Somebody just called, looking for her, too. Hey," he added, more sharply now, "I bet that was you, wasn't it?"

I couldn't think of a plausible reason to deny it. "It's quite important that I find her," I said. "Do you know where she is this weekend?"

The two of them exchanged a look. I had the feeling they were deciding to stonewall me just as effectively as the police had done. I wasn't getting any fonder of the feeling as the day wore on.

"How come it's any of your business?" the first man asked.

31

I didn't have a plausible answer to that, either. This detecting job wasn't so simple after all, I realized, especially if you had scruples about lying. I had to fall back on the truth, although I wasn't happy sharing it with these two obviously hostile young men.

"Her boyfriend called me for a tow last night, but he was gone when I showed up," I said. "Somebody said he and Jeri had gone away for the weekend. I'm trying to—"

I didn't get to finish. There was a simultaneous snarl from both men, and the first one banged his palm forcefully against a kitchen table that looked only barely up to the challenge.

"She better not be!" he roared. "She just better not be anywhere near him, that's all."

The second man was moving closer to me now, and it was hard to stand my ground. "You're not telling us the whole story," he said. "Are you?"

He sounded distinctly threatening. "I'm telling you what I know," I said. "There's no need to be—"

"Yeah, there is!" The second man was shouting now, too. "She's got no business being with that Tom Wilson. Got it?"

"Hey, I've got it." I didn't, though, not quite. "What's so bad about Tom Wilson, anyway?" I couldn't resist adding.

The two men—they had to be Jeri's brothers, I thought—stared at each other for a moment, as though they couldn't imagine anyone not knowing what was so bad about Tom Wilson. "Even if the guy *wasn't* some kind of criminal—" the first brother said, and then stopped.

"*Is* he some kind of criminal?" I tried not to look as interested as I felt.

The brothers were quieter after their initial outburst, but there was something sulkily angry about them that I didn't like. I wished they would just tell me what they knew, so I could get out of there.

"He used to be in the police log all the time," the second brother said. "Picking fights with people. Getting in trouble."

"And?" That clearly wasn't the whole story.

"Jeri just shouldn't be around somebody like that, that's all."

I looked at the two men. I could quite easily imagine them picking fights with people and getting in trouble. If there were ever a case of the pot calling the kettle black—

The word *black* finally made the connection in my head. "Wait a minute," I said. "Is Tom Wilson black?"

They nodded sullenly, without speaking. They clearly weren't about to admit to me that they didn't want their sister dating a black guy, but just as clearly, that was what was making them so angry.

I thought about the silent, shadowy figure on my lot last night, and tried not to let my glance stray to the well-developed muscles of the brother nearest to me. These guys obviously hated Tom Wilson—or at least the color of his skin— and they hated the idea of their sister being involved with him. Did that hatred extend to trying to make off with his truck in the night? Had Jeri perhaps said something to her brothers about buying a painting that might be worth a lot of money? I decided I was going to have to think hard about the Crozier brothers and what part they might have played in all this.

Tonight wasn't the time to think about that, or about much else. I still had the barbecued chicken I had picked up at Shop 'n Save with me, and I drove it to my son Mike's house, where food is always welcomed. Mike is single at twenty-six, and spends most of his waking hours underneath cars—by day, at Adams Chevrolet in the center of Athol and after hours, in his garage at home. When he comes up for air, he's usually hungry.

"Smells good," he said, when I dangled the foil bag under the car he was working on at the moment. "You been cooking?"

"Not me. It's from the nice people at Shop 'n Save."

Mike made some more appreciative noises, and added, "What's it going to cost me?"

"You're a very cynical young man," I said.

He snorted and wheeled himself out from under the car. "You want me to revive the damn tow truck again, don't you?" he asked.

"It has a bad cough," I admitted. "If I can get it through the rest of the weekend, I'll be finding out on Monday whether I'm getting that loan or not. And if I am—"

"There'll be a whole new truck for me to work on when I should be fixing other people's cars for money." Mike finished the sentence for me and wiped his hands. "Come on. Let's go eat."

Hannah would have given me a long lecture by now about trying to run the towing business by myself, or about being out when I should have been resting, or about any number of things that weren't quite right with my life. Mike never lectured me. I could see in his eyes that he had serious doubts about how much longer Henry's Towing was going to exist, but—mercifully—he didn't feel the need to share those doubts with me. We ate dinner in friendly silence and later he tinkered with the tow truck until it stopped wheezing. I drove home in it shortly after dark.

I stopped at Belanger's Package Store in the center of Orange on my way home. My headache had calmed down for the moment, but I was bone weary and feeling the need of a little pampering. I've said I don't like other people fussing over me, but occasionally I do fuss over myself. It usually takes the form of a glass of Tia Maria and an early bed.

The problem was, my supply of Tia Maria was low. I stopped by the automatic teller at the Athol Savings Bank and then drove to Orange. I pulled the truck into the municipal parking lot just down the hill from Belanger's and walked into the store expecting only the usual friendly greeting and maybe a comment or two about my taste in liquor which tends to run toward the sweet and sticky. There are more than a few people in my life who consider my palate to be uneducated.

I got the comments I'd been expecting and some sympathy as well about last night's misadventure. But as Terri Belanger was ringing up my bottle at the cash register, I got something else, too: another piece of the puzzle I was working on, involving the missing Tom Wilson and his pickup truck and his girlfriend, Jeri Crozier.

TERRI BELANGER

Belanger's is a comfortably cluttered place with coolers on one wall and bottles on the other and big inflatable items—an over-sized baseball glove, a raft, a dinosaur—in all the corners. Behind the counter there were long strips of lottery tickets. My eye was caught by them this evening, probably because they were bright and shiny and I was so tired, but once I'd looked in that direction, I saw something else that wakened me up in a hurry.

It was a newspaper clipping, with a photograph of a slender dark-haired girl being handed what was, judging by her expression, a rather large check. It wasn't the picture that captured my attention, but the caption underneath. The name was Jeri Crozier.

I was so intent on reading it that I completely forgot Terri Belanger was holding my change out to me. I took it finally and nodded at the clipping. "Did she buy the ticket here?" I asked.

Terri nodded. "Last month," she confirmed. "I never saw anybody so excited. She said she'd been planning for months what she would do if she ever won any money." She grinned. "Of course, most of us would probably have some ideas on that subject, I guess."

"I know I would." I could easily have found a home for an extra twenty-five hundred dollars, the amount the newspaper caption announced Jeri Crozier had won, but for once, my mind wasn't anywhere near my own money woes. I was thinking instead about the coincidence of Jeri having won the money right before she and her boyfriend had taken off on a special trip. What had they had in mind? What had they suddenly been able to afford to do? Did any of this have to do with the painting they had bought, the one they'd thought might be worth a lot?

I thanked Terri and drove home, not sure now what my next step should be.

It has always been my belief that any decision is more reliable if you make it on a full stomach. And so the next morning

I had a shower, carefully shampooing around the bump on my head. I put on my work clothes and headed to Woody's.

Woody's Main Street Diner in Athol is my favorite breakfast place, because it's friendly and affordable and I nearly always run into somebody I know there. The diner is small, just a single row of stools at a long counter with Woody and two waitresses behind it, and on this Saturday morning I got the very last seat, which happened to be next to Kay Gleason, who happens to be in the antiques trade. I didn't know her well, but well enough to say hello and to know that she runs Historical Ink, a business dealing in historical maps. I thought about the local landscape painting Tom Wilson and his girlfriend had wanted to have valued on Thursday evening and decided that it was fate, and not just hunger, that had prompted me to come to Woody's this morning.

I ordered coffee and eggs and roast-beef hash—Woody's roast-beef hash is another reason I patronize the diner—and managed to get into a friendly, general, Saturday-morning-type conversation with Kay and her daughter Beckie on the subject of local painters.

"Are there any local landscape painters whose work might be worth something?" I asked. "Anything that might be likely to show up in somebody's shop around here, for instance?"

Kay took a sip of her coffee. "I'm not really the one to ask," she said. "Are you shopping, Rita?"

"Sort of." Shopping for answers, I thought, and for clues to the whereabouts of a young man and his girlfriend. I couldn't get rid of a lingering concern about Tom and Jeri, somehow. Maybe it was the threat in Jeri's brothers' voices or the image of the abandoned red pickup truck on a rainy night. Whatever was causing it, I couldn't get over the sense that something wrong here, that the two young people who had been planning a weekend away might have ended up with something different than they'd bargained for.

Kay gave me some names of some local antique dealers who might know about landscape painters, and I scribbled them down on my napkin.

"You might also want to try across the street at the book-store," Beckie Gleason added. "They've got some local history books there. I don't think there's one just on painters, but there might be something that would give you some ideas."

"Thanks," I said and finished off my coffee in one swallow. Jim's Auto was going to be picking up my towing calls until this afternoon, and I had just decided how I would fill in the time before I was scheduled to go to work again.

BECKIE GLEASON

KAY GLEASON

FIVE

I started with Harbour Books just east of Woody's diner on Main Street. Harbour Books is far more eclectic than your average bookstore: it sells toys and tapes and jewelry and cards, all crammed into an old two-story house. It's chaotic and entertaining and congenial, with the flavor of a kind of New Age general store.

The porch was bright with Halloween banners and kids' costumes this Saturday morning. There were plenty of customers inside browsing through books, checking out posters, or playing with the little cross-eyed brown tabby cat that lived at the store and could often be found sleeping in unlikely corners.

"Our local books are over here," the owner said. "What exactly are you looking for?"

Part of the problem was that I didn't know. "General information about local painters, I guess," I said. "I'm trying to identify a painting."

He started pulling books off the shelf and handing them to me. "There might be something in here," he said. "And this one is just a general history of the area. That might help. Have you talked to any of the antique dealers around here?"

I said I was about to do that. He suggested a couple of names that weren't on Kay Gleason's list and added, "We can special-order anything you like if you can find a title that might help you."

"Thanks." I was looking through the books he'd handed me and not coming up with anything. As I put them back on the shelf, a familiar name caught my eye. Between a fat history of the Quabbin Reservoir and a slimmer book on the mills of Pelham, I saw the title *Inventors and their Inventions in Orange and Athol* by McGarrity Brooks.

"Do you know him?" The bookstore owner had followed my gaze.

"Slightly."

"He keeps saying he's going to publish a bigger book about tools, but it never seems to get finished," the owner said. "How about a poster? You like art. You should look at the new post-

41

ers we just got in. There's some Van Gogh, and some Star Trek, right over here."

I said I wasn't interested in Van Gogh, or Star Trek. I bought a couple of cards while I was there, though, and said hello to Chloe the cat before leaving the store. If I was going to get to all the antique dealers on my list, I thought, I had better get moving.

It's funny how you don't see things until you have a reason to look for them. I've never been much interested in antiques—Henry and I inherited a lot of old furniture from his parents, and I've spent a lot of effort trying to keep it from falling apart over the years. When your only set of chairs needs its spindles doctored every time you sit down, or when you have to come up with strategic ways to move the centerpiece on the dining room table around to flatten the veneer you've just re-glued for the umpteenth time, shopping for more old furniture doesn't have any particular appeal.

So I'd never really noticed just how many antique places there were in our area until I started calling on the names Kay Gleason had given me. I started in at the top of the list, with Memories Antiques on Route 2A between Athol and Orange.

The owner Bev Starkey showed me around her shop, which had started out as half of a two-car garage. Bev told me it had expanded from there. I wished I had more time to look around the place: there were dozens and dozens of key-shaped thermometers hanging from the roof supports and shelves of glassware lining the walls. There were more antique buttons than I had ever seen in once place, some in loose bins, some sewn to cards. Bev was sorting through more buttons as we talked.

"We have a few paintings," she said. "Mostly what you see on the walls here."

"What I'm actually after," I said, "is some information about a young couple who apparently bought a local landscape a little while ago. They were in their early twenties. He was black. She was white."

Mixed-race couples are still unusual in our part of the state. That has its attendant problems—the reactions of Jeri's broth-

BEV STARKEY

ers being a typical example—but for the purposes of my investigation, it could be a big plus that they were so recognizable. And it was: Bev Starkey was nodding even before I had finished speaking.

"Oh, yes, I remember them," she said. "They were just browsing, they said. A couple of weeks ago. A Saturday, I think—that's when most people do their looking around. I had the feeling they were setting up house together and looking for inexpensive antiques. The girl seemed very excited about old things."

I was surprised at how pleased I was—not that Jeri was excited about old things, but that I'd managed to pick up the trail so quickly. Bev was telling me now that Haley's Antiques in Athol was a good bet for information on paintings, and I thanked her and got back in the wrecker.

I'd driven by Haley's for years without ever going in. The business filled two buildings: a red wooden barn full of books and chairs and prints and picture frames and odds and ends, and an old slate-roofed white house that clearly held the more valuable merchandise. Both places were full of browsers on this Saturday morning, but it was easy to get the attention of the owner. She was sitting at a computer that looked alien in the middle of a big room with a parquet floor and old exposed beams.

I asked her the same questions I'd asked Bev Starkey and got almost the same answers. "I remember them," the proprietor said. "They were looking for inexpensive stuff—to furnish an old farmhouse, they said."

"Were they buying a farmhouse?" I asked.

"I'm not sure. They bought a painting from me, and the young woman seemed excited about it because she said it looked exactly like the place they were planning to move into."

As casually as I could, I said, "I don't suppose the painting was worth a great deal, was it?"

"It was worth a hundred bucks, which is what I charged them," the woman said. "It wouldn't have been worth that much, except that it had cows in it."

"Cows?"

"Cows make a farm scene more valuable. People like pictures with cows."

"Do you know who painted it?"

"It wasn't signed. It came out of a lot I bought at an auction. Somebody painted it a while ago, and it had been up in the attic nearly that long."

"Would you be willing to give me the name of the people who had the auction?" I asked.

The woman's glance had sharpened with each question I'd asked. "You're awfully interested in an anonymous painting," she commented.

I considered my options in a hurry. Once again, as with the Crozier brothers, it seemed that the simple truth was the best way to go. "Someone told me the young couple thought the painting might actually be valuable," I said.

The proprietor laughed. "Trust me," she said, "it wasn't. If it had been a James Franklin Gilman or somebody like that, I wouldn't have been selling it for a hundred bucks out of my barn."

"Who's James Franklin Gilman?"

"An itinerant painter in the late eighteenth century. He worked in the Athol area. Every five years, Polly Whipps organizes Gilman shows at the Athol Historical Society. Occasionally one of his things turns up on the market."

"What would a James Franklin Gilman painting be worth?"

"You're a very persistent lady."

I didn't tell her I already knew that. You have to be a persistent lady to run a towing business by yourself for eight years. If I hadn't been a persistent lady, I wouldn't still be following the trail of Tom Wilson and Jeri Crozier and their mysterious painting. I didn't say any of that but just waited for an answer.

"Five grand," she said finally. "More or less. But this wasn't a Gilman, believe me. Or anything else remotely valuable."

"Could there have been another painting underneath it?" I asked. "Painted on the same canvas? Doesn't that sometimes happen?"

"Often enough that most dealers have a black-light box that we check paintings against. This was nothing but a simple landscape with cows."

There was a shrewdness in the way she spoke that made me believe she knew what she was doing. But where, then, had Tom Wilson gotten the idea that his painting was worth a lot of money? Had it been pure wishful thinking? And if he'd been taking it to McGarrity Brooks to be appraised, had the painting been in the truck—behind the seat, maybe—when I'd arrived? In which case, where was it now? Had that been what someone had been after when the pickup truck's window had been smashed two nights ago?

"Do you know McGarrity Brooks?" I asked the woman from Haley's.

She nodded. "Slightly," she said. "We're both in the Rotary Club, although he hasn't been to many meetings lately."

"What's your opinion of him? As a dealer, I mean."

"McGarrity is—" She seemed to have to search for the right phrase. "He's as *persnickety* as they come," she said finally. "A nicer way to put it would be to say that he's exceptionally thorough."

"So he knows what he's doing? Would he be able to give a dependable valuation of, say, a painting?"

"Oh, he's solid enough. Why do you ask?"

"The young couple who bought that painting from you were taking it to him to be appraised."

She shrugged. "He would give them an accurate appraisal," she said. "*If* he could drag his attention away from that tome he's writing on antique tools. It's his retirement project, he says, which is why he almost never gets out to auctions and shows any more."

"Was he by any chance at the auction where you bought the local landscape?" I wasn't sure where I was going with this line of thought. It just seemed important to check out whatever I could while I had the attention of this knowledgeable and gregarious antique dealer.

Unfortunately, her attention was already shifting to a woman who stood in the doorway with a blue vase and a checkbook in her hand. And my luck on questioning seemed to have run out, too.

"McGarrity hasn't been anywhere for the last few months," she said. "He was in the hospital for heart trouble, and he's been recuperating since July or so. Now, if you'll excuse me, I have to sell a vase to this blue-and-white china collector, Ellen Hargis."

She turned to the next customer, and I took the hint. "If you could just give me the name of the people who had that auction," I said, as I moved toward the door.

She was already dealing with the blue vase, peeling off the price sticker, reaching for a sheet of newsprint to wrap it up. "Harrison, I think," she said, over her shoulder. "It might have been Horrigan. I didn't pay much attention, to tell you the truth. It was at an auction gallery, in Greenfield."

I thanked her, and said goodbye. Well, McGarrity Brooks might be a dead end, but I wasn't out of options yet. I had a name—Harrison, or maybe Horrigan—and I still had more names on my list of antique dealers with enough time to find out whether that they might have been at the same auction. I was beginning to feel quite proud of my amateur detective work.

By mid-afternoon my luck seemed to have run out. I'd talked to Gary Moise, who owned the Orange Trading Company, an old mill building on the river in Orange. Gary had converted the big building to a cooperative antique business, with dealers' booths on the ground floor and bigger things—architectural salvage items and old lunch-counter fittings and Gary's specialties, jukeboxes and slot machines, upstairs.

He thought hard and said he vaguely remembered the auction being advertised, although he hadn't gone.

"I don't go to many auctions," he said. "Not unless they're selling jukeboxes or unless I had some personal connection with the owners. I seem to remember there were lots of books in that sale, though. Why don't you call Ed Rumrill, up in North Orange? He specializes in old books."

So I headed up to North Orange. To get there, I had to drive right past the place where Tom Wilson's pickup truck had skidded off the road on Thursday night. Just before I came to the place, I noticed the helpful neighbor who'd let Tom and Jeri use his phone, and I made a sudden decision to pull over and

GARY MOISE

call to him, "Did you by any chance ever hear from that young couple whose truck went off the road a couple of nights ago?"

The bearded man was out raking his lawn, and he looked surprised to see me. "Why would I have heard from them?" he asked.

"I thought they might have come back and wondered where their truck had gotten to."

He shook his head. "I haven't heard a thing," he said.

Further up the road, I could still see skid marks where the pickup truck had plowed into the soft ground under the trees. "Where are you, Tom and Jeri?" I said out loud. It was much less unnerving to be alone out here in the daylight, even though it was still overcast and raining fitfully. But there was something about the scene that made me uneasy just the same.

I thought about the young couple and their apparent plans to move into an old farmhouse together. But they hadn't had any money to speak of: I remembered Tom Wilson's neighbor commenting that he had once been deeply in debt, although he was almost clear of it now. And Jeri had her lottery winnings, but twenty-five hundred bucks certainly didn't buy you a future these days.

Had they been counting on their painting to pay for their plans? Or did they have something else in mind? I'd come up with all kinds of improbable schemes myself while trying to figure out how to keep Henry's Towing solvent, and had ended up discarding all my ideas because they'd been either dangerous or illegal, more often both.

I wondered if Tom and Jeri had been thinking along those lines. I was beginning to like my mental picture of the two young people: hard-working, in love despite antagonism from their co-workers and Jeri's brothers, dreaming of a future together. I hoped that in trying to bankroll that future, they hadn't gotten into something that meant real trouble.

I'd been idling at the side of the road, mulling all this over, but a passing car reminded me that I was supposed to be on my way to see Ed Rumrill's antique book business in North Orange. Before I went, though, I wanted to pay one more visit to McGarrity Brooks, just up the road.

There was a car in the driveway, and I could hear voices from the living room. I knocked anyway.

"Oh, yes, Mrs.—Magritte, isn't it?" McGarrity Brooks peered out at me. "Can I help you?"

"I hope so," I said. "I had a couple more questions about the young people who were coming to you for an appraisal on Thursday. But if you've got company—"

By then McGarrity had the screen door open and I had stepped through it. I've learned if you say all the right polite things in the right tone of voice—like "Oh, don't let me interrupt you"—you can be as pushy as you like and no one will notice.

McGarrity Brooks certainly didn't seem to. He ushered me in to the living room, and introduced his guest as the owner of Spaulding Graphics. "We're just discussing my book," he said. "On the products of the local tool mills."

"Your ten-volume set of books, you mean." The graphic designer didn't sound nearly as pleased about the project as McGarrity was. "Mr. Brooks, in all honesty, I can't give you a quote until I know how much material you're going to want to include."

"Surely just a rough estimate—"

"Would be pretty unrealistic. Try to understand. I know it seems important to you to put in everything you've done. But you've obviously spent a lifetime on this research, and I can't possibly tell you how much it would take to design the book until you've distilled your material into some kind of useable form. I'm sorry, but we can't do business until then."

McGarrity Brooks' manner changed slightly. He and the woman from Spaulding Graphics had obviously been sitting on his sofa looking at a prodigious stack of paper, photographs, and a few loose tools on the table in front of them. Some of the display cases were open, I noticed. Now he stood up again, frowning.

"I'm not sure we can do business at all," he said, crisply. "This book demands a great deal of sympathy from the designer. I've interviewed several local companies, and I'm sorry to say I haven't found one yet who seems to understand what I'm trying to do."

The look on the woman's face suggested that she understood better than McGarrity did what he was trying to do. "I'm sorry, Mr. Brooks," she said. "I try to go out of my way to help writers get their books into print, but this just isn't ready for a designer to deal with yet. I'll be happy to give you a quote when you get your materials into some shape I can look at."

When the woman had gone, McGarrity tossed her business card on top of the pile of paper. "Spaulding Graphics came highly recommended," he said, as if I'd recommended the company and he wanted me to know what he thought of my judgement. "They did a book that I heard good things about, last year."

He mentioned the name, and I recognized it, because I had seen it on the local history shelf at Harbour Books. I remembered being impressed by the appearance of the book, and contrasted that with the morass of loose paper on McGarrity's living room table. I tried to imagine organizing it into a single volume and decided I would put my money on the professionalism of Spaulding Graphics any day. McGarrity Brooks might be thorough, as the owner of Haley's Antiques had told me, but he was clearly also impossible to work with.

Fortunately, I didn't have to work with him. I had two questions to ask him, that was all.

"I wondered if you had any idea why Tom Wilson thought his painting was valuable," I said.

"Tom Wilson? Was that his full name? He really didn't give me any idea, I'm afraid. Just said he had a hunch he'd gotten a real bargain, and would I check it out."

I asked my last question anyway. "I don't suppose you've heard anything from him since Thursday night," I said.

"No, of course not. In fact, except for that graphic designer and yourself, I haven't heard from anyone at all since Thursday night. Unless, of course, you count whoever it was who broke into my shop early Friday morning."

I blinked. "What time Friday morning?" I asked.

"About three-thirty A.M. They smashed a shop window and went inside."

Suddenly my dead end had opened up again. "Would you mind," I said slowly, "telling me more?"

SIX

There wasn't a lot more to tell. The shop, McGarrity Brooks said, was behind his house, in what had once been the garage. "It wasn't a serious break-in, probably just some kids out to break a window for fun. Not that I can understand why that should be fun, but—"

I broke in. "So nothing was taken?" I said. I was thinking of the sound of tinkling glass on the pavement of my side lot, when my unknown intruder had smashed the window of Tom Wilson's truck.

"Not as far as I can tell."

"Would you be willing to show me?" I asked.

"Yes, of course." McGarrity fished a key ring out of his pocket. I remembered how eager he had been to mention his book on tools when I'd arrived; I had the same impression again now. He seemed to think his own affairs were so important that it didn't surprise him to have passing strangers inquiring about the break-in at his shop.

He was right, it wasn't very dramatic. A window in the big garage door had been smashed in, and the space was covered with plywood now. Whoever had done it had apparently reached in and opened the lock, McGarrity explained, but aside from a few papers being mussed up, there didn't seem to be anything missing.

"A mindless prank," he said. "Annoying, of course, and a little frightening. I'm planning to have an alarm system installed as a result of it, I can tell you. But the police didn't seem to think I should worry unduly."

I wondered whether I should tell him that someone had broken into my place, too, the same night. That probably *would* worry him unduly, and I remembered the woman at Haley's telling me that McGarrity had had heart trouble this summer. If nothing had been taken, then presumably it was because whoever had broken in had discovered that there was nothing to take—at least, not the thing the intruder was looking for.

And what was that? I was becoming more and more certain that it had to be the painting Tom and Jeri had bought for a hundred dollars at Haley's. What was it about the painting that was apparently driving some unknown person to break through windows and chain-link fences to get to it?

"Are you sure about the time of the break-in?" I asked McGarrity Brooks.

"Absolutely. I heard the glass break, and looked at my bedside clock at almost exactly three-thirty. The clock is very accurate. I've had it for years, and I've never known it to deviate from the correct time."

Persnickety, I thought. That was, beyond doubt, the word for old McGarrity. But it was handy, too, to have a witness so clear about his facts.

He didn't have any more facts to tell me, beyond the obvious one that he used his former garage as an all-purpose work space, where he sold occasional antiques and restored old tools and wrote up his all-too-copious notes for the book he wanted to publish.

"Some of these are quite valuable," he said, picking up a small plane and running a finger carefully along its side. "Of course, I have the most collectible of them up in the house. It's a good thing the thief didn't know that."

I felt quite sure the thief didn't care. Furthermore, I felt sure whoever had broken in here had not found what he—or she—wanted, and so had headed over to my place.

I puzzled over it as I got back into the truck. I wondered if by some stretch of the imagination, someone who sold alarm systems was trying to drum up as much business as possible by scaring first McGarrity Brooks and then me into buying electronic watchdogs just as soon as we could. It wasn't a great theory, but it was the best I could come up with at the moment.

The afternoon was wearing on, and soon I was going to have to turn my beeper back on and start taking the towing calls that are always most numerous on wet Saturday nights. I wanted to get to the book dealer in North Orange first, if I could, and then maybe back home for a quick lunch before I went back to work.

ED RUMRILL

Ed Rumrill was in his shop, which occupied the back part of his old white farmhouse. And he was more than happy to tell me what I wanted to know.

"Sure," he said, "I remember that auction. Got a lot of good stuff there, old military books, mostly. They must have had a military buff in that family."

"Do you remember the family name?" I asked hopefully.

"Let me think. I don't generally pay much attention to that end of things, to be honest with you. And I had two auctions to go to that day. Sullivan, maybe? Sheridan?"

"How about Harrison?" I suggested. "Or Horrigan?"

"Could have been. Hooligan, maybe. No, that doesn't sound right. But it was something like that."

Great, I thought. Some three-syllable name, that might start with an H, or maybe an S. I looked through the shelf of military volumes that Ed Rumrill pointed out to me, wondering how on earth anybody could think of so much to say about the first World War. I was about to thank him and take my leave when he remembered something else.

"Paul Blanchard was there, too," he said. "You know—he runs Paul's Place in Athol. You might want to check with him, see if he remembers the name."

"I'll do that," I said.

I figured I just had time, and headed back to Athol again. I detected a slight wheeziness when I drove uphill in the tow truck and remembered Mike telling me that all the starting and stopping was what was wearing out the starter. "Sorry," I muttered to the truck. "Hang on until Monday, and then maybe we'll be able to get you a younger brother to do most of the work."

I got to Athol by two-thirty, but I never did get to see Paul Blanchard that day. I was heading into town on Exchange Street, through the light at Main and was on my way to Paul's Place on South Street when I saw Tom and Jeri.

Not in the flesh, but close enough to make me tromp on the brakes and startle the driver behind me. On the left hand side of Exchange there was a photography studio called Robert Mayer Photography. There were various display pictures in the window—a wedding portrait, a pair of smiling kids, and a small round object I couldn't quite make out, except that it looked vaguely like a turtle.

I backed into a parking space in front of the Athol-Clinton Co-operative Bank and hurried across the street. The small round object turned out to be a kitten—a pedigreed one, presumably, if someone had commissioned its portrait. But it wasn't the kitten that interested me. It was the photograph of a smiling young couple, seated together on a wooden bench. He was black, she was white, and they looked very pleased to be together and having their picture taken. And the young woman, at least, looked very familiar. I had last seen her face in the newspaper photograph at Belanger's Package Store.

The sign on Robert Mayer's door said "Closed," but when I peered through to the back of the shop, I could see a light on and hear sounds. I knocked, and after a moment a man appeared with a black and white contact sheet in his hand.

I gave him my best smile—the grandmotherly one—and pointed at the portrait in the window. The owner unlocked the door and told me he'd just been working in his darkroom and was about to go out and photograph a wedding. He spared a few minutes, though, to add that he had just put Tom and Jeri's picture on display that morning. "You don't often get engagement pictures where both parties look so happy," he told me.

"I didn't know they were engaged."

"Are they friends of yours?"

"No. Yes. Well, sort of." I wasn't quite as slick at this interrogation business as I'd been starting to think. The fact was that I still didn't have a completely rock-solid reason to be going around checking up on Tom Wilson and Jeri Crozier, unless you counted the bump on my head as rock-solid. But the truth was also that I was getting more and more intrigued by the mystery I seemed to have landed in the middle of.

"Well," the photographer was saying, "I suppose I could tell a sort-of friend that they went away to Las Vegas this weekend to get married. They said it had been kind of a secret, but they told me that as of today I could go ahead and tell the world, if

I wanted to. So I put the picture on display. They were a nice young couple. Very sweet together."

"Did you happen to know either of them before you took their picture?"

"Never met them. Why?"

I was trying to reconcile what I had heard about Tom Wilson—that he'd been seriously in debt and frequently in the police log for fighting—with my own impression of him. I was getting a picture of a young man trying to clean up his act, but being trailed by a reputation he'd grown out of. I wondered what else might be trailing him or Jeri. I already knew about a couple of angry brothers and a resentful ex-boyfriend at Baker School Specialty. Would that explain Tom and Jeri's secrecy about their engagement and the weekend away to get married?

Had they gotten married, after all? Or had something happened to them to prevent it? I was increasingly concerned, even though I knew it wasn't really my business. My kids always told me I let my curiosity get the better of me, and I was beginning to realize just how right they were.

The photographer didn't know any more than he'd already told me, though, and I knew it was time to go. Before I left, I looked around his small showroom, admiring some exceptionally appealing portraits of children—some with prize ribbons on them—and a complicated arrangement of gears and cogs and bits that might have been an engine before it became an ingenious work of art.

"It must be a nice change to take pictures of machines," I said. "They stay right where you've posed them."

He laughed. "You're right. And they don't complain after that their chin doesn't really look that way, either." His smile faded. "Although the owner of this particular engine didn't feel I'd quite done it justice."

"I can't imagine why not." I looked at the picture again. "I think it's fascinating."

"Thanks. This particular guy is pretty hard to satisfy, that's all."

The comment rang a bell. "His name wouldn't be McGarrity Brooks, by any chance, would it?" I asked.

"As a matter of fact, it would. He wanted to hire me to photograph some old tools he's writing a book on. We couldn't agree on a price, and I offered to do a few shots on spec, because the project intrigued me. This was the best of them, but apparently it wasn't what Mr. Brooks had in mind. How do you know him?"

"Chance acquaintance," I said. I didn't want to go into a lot of detail about Tom and Jeri and the pickup truck and the bump on my head. And I had just about enough time to get to Paul's Place before I had to go to work. I thanked Mr. Mayer for letting me in even when he was supposed to be off duty and headed back across the street.

When I got back into the tow truck, though, my beeper was going off I called my service from a pay phone outside Victory Supermarket and found I'd been called to an accident down in New Salem. "Right in the center of town," my answering service said. "Just past the sign for Ann Clukay-Whittier's law office. You can't miss it."

I didn't miss it, but I did miss my chance to talk to Paul Blanchard that day, and that meant it took an extra half day for me to piece together everything I'd learned so far and figure out just what was going on around me. And by the time I did, it had progressed from being merely dangerous to being downright deadly.

SEVEN

It was a busy night, as I'd expected. But at least the weather cleared gradually, and by midnight there was a brilliant half-moon overhead.

My last call was at two A.M., to tow a car that had quit on Route 32 in front of Mann Lumber. "It's been sounding kind of funny lately," the driver said, as I fitted the blocks carefully around his bumper. Newer tow trucks came with a different kind of fitting that was easier to use and less likely to damage a towed car, but my old wrecker was out-of-date enough that I still had to fuss with wooden blocks. It was one of the many things I wouldn't miss if I got my loan. "I hoped it would last through the weekend," the driver added.

"I know," I said. "Denial is great, isn't it?" I hoped he wouldn't notice the asthmatic sounds my own truck was making as I pulled away from the side of the road.

I'd been back to my house a couple of times during the night, and once I'd seen a state police car cruising slowly and purposefully past the place. Chili Dog had barked at it, but half-heartedly, as though he knew these were the good guys and was just making the point that he was on duty, too. Tom Wilson's red pickup truck was still there with the thick sheet of plastic I'd taped in place still covering the passenger side window.

"You still owe me thirty bucks for the tow, buddy," I said to the absent Tom Wilson. "Not to mention the storage fees and the bump on the head."

I was too tired to puzzle over it any more today. I said good-night to Henry's caricature, fell into bed, and slept without dreaming until ten the next morning.

Sunday was gloriously sunny, and although the rain had knocked a lot of the autumn leaves off, there was enough color left to make everything seem bright and airy. I thought about sleeping in, but Chili Dog is always ravenous in the mornings and over the past eight years I've become programmed to get up and give him his breakfast as soon as I'm awake.

Strangely, I didn't hear him making his usual "Feed me" noises when I got to the back step. Generally he bounds out of his doghouse and runs to meet me. Generally he forgets, too, that there's a limit to how far his chain will let him go, and then he barks indignantly, as though someone was conspiring to keep him from getting anything to eat ever again.

This morning, though, I could see him still sleeping inside the doghouse. I called him, and he raised his head slightly, but then he put it back down again. I could hear him snoring before I got halfway across the yard.

"Chili?" I said. "You all right, big guy?"

He sighed, wheezed, and lifted his eyelids briefly. He was clearly sound asleep, dreaming. At first I thought he must be sick, and then I noticed the bones.

There were three of them, big steak bones, judging by what Chili had left of them. They were thoroughly chewed, lying just in front of the doghouse. He couldn't have gotten them out of someone's garbage, I realized. His chain was still clipped securely to his collar.

If Chili hadn't gone out and gotten the bones, that meant someone had brought the bones to Chili. There wasn't any other explanation.

I felt suddenly cold. Someone must have been here in the night, silencing my watchdog with meat that—judging from the stupor he was in this morning—must have been drugged. They'd put Chili to sleep, to keep him from sounding the alarm.

Later, I was able to feel grateful that at least they hadn't killed him, but at the moment I was too upset at the idea that my property had been invaded again, for a reason I still didn't understand.

Chili Dog was struggling to his feet now, apparently interested in a squirrel climbing a nearby pine tree, so I decided he was coming out from under whatever he had been fed. I spent some time reassuring myself, and then I hustled over to the car lot, heading straight for Tom Wilson's truck.

I could see that the hastily-repaired chain-link fence around the lot had been cut open again, and the plastic over the red pickup's window was disturbed, too. I opened the door and looked inside, muttering that this was crazy, that there was absolutely nothing left to steal in this truck. I'd checked it over myself.

For a moment I thought everything looked just the same, except for the torn plastic hanging from the window frame. And then I saw the picture.

It was stuffed far under the seat, and I could only see a corner of it. It was wrapped in a dark plastic garbage bag, and taped securely shut. When I'd pulled it out and gotten rid of the plastic, though, there wasn't a lot of doubt about what I was looking at. The colors were dark and dingy. The painting was distinctly amateur-looking, but the farm scene with brown and white cows grazing contentedly in front of a red barn was almost certainly the painting that Tom and Jeri had bought at Haley's Antiques.

"This doesn't make sense," I said out loud. "Why would someone break in—again—to put a painting *back* in the truck?"

I restored the chain-link fence as well as I could, and took the painting inside. I felt I needed caffeine if I was going to figure this new development out.

Even two cups of extra strong coffee didn't do the trick, though. Maybe someone had hoped to steal the painting and sell it while Tom and Jeri were away, only to discover that it really wasn't worth anything, after all. That theory made the most sense, but it didn't tell me who was behind all this, or why they had bothered to return the painting.

I called the state police to report this latest wrinkle. The officer I talked to told me the obvious explanation was that I'd simply overlooked the painting the first time I had checked over the truck.

"I can *guarantee* it wasn't there before," I said.

The state trooper made a noncommittal noise, meaning, I interpreted, that he didn't believe me. "You had a bad bump on your head there, Mrs. Magritte," he said soothingly. "You're entitled to be a little fuzzy on some of the details for a while." He told me they would make a note of it, but I had a feeling it wasn't going to prompt any kind of immediate action.

Which meant it was still up to me to find out what was happening and why. I tried calling the woman at Haley's Antiques and got an answering machine. I thought about visiting Paul's Place, the store I hadn't gotten to yesterday, but they probably didn't open until noon on Sundays. So I spent the morning puzzling in solitude, trying to work things through, and eventually, when Chili Dog was fully awake, dragging him for a vigorous walk that perked him up again and worked off some of my excess energy.

I was at Paul's Place even before it opened, and I talked to Paul Blanchard as he was putting out some display items in his parking lot—a couple of kids' bikes and some wooden laundry racks.

"Sure, I remember that auction," he said. "I got a lot of used furniture there—dressers, mostly, and a couple of sideboards. They're upstairs if you want to take a look."

I told him I was more interested in the previous owners than in their furniture. "Do you remember the name of the family, by any chance?" I asked.

"The name? I'd have to think about it." I held my breath while he thought, willing him to come up with it.

Miraculously, he did, after thirty seconds or so. "Sorrigan," he said positively. "That was it. An older couple, I forget their first names. They live up on one of those roads that leads into Warwick, just before the center of town."

"You've just made my day," I said and left him looking puzzled about how he had managed to do that.

It wasn't hard to find the Sorrigans. Their names weren't in the phone book, but one of the advantages of being a tow truck driver is you get to know all the highways and byways where you live. I had been up and down "those roads leading into Warwick" many times, and I took a ride up there now, looking hard at mailboxes.

Warwick is a picturesque, rural Massachusetts town with a small central cluster of old wooden buildings and several roads radiating out from the center. It only took me three tries to find the house I was looking for. An elderly couple was out raking leaves; both were tall and white-haired, and the man looked slightly familiar.

PAUL BLANCHARD

"Oh, yes, that's one of Uncle William's paintings," the woman said, after I'd introduced myself and pulled out the painting that had mysteriously returned itself to Tom Wilson's pickup truck. "There were several of them, just like that one."

"He painted the same scene?" I asked.

"Over and over. It seemed to make him happy. We saved one out for each of Charlie's sisters, when we emptied out the old house, and a couple of neighbors wanted them, too. Come on inside, and I'll show you the one we kept."

The couple told me they were Charles and Dorothy Sorrigan and that they had recently cleaned out Charlie's great-uncle's farmhouse after the old man had died at the age of ninety-nine. "Uncle William was a bit of a recluse—he said he'd seen enough of the world when he was in Europe during the First World War," Charlie Sorrigan said. "He came home to Warwick and announced his intentions of staying here for the rest of his life. Plus when he got home, he discovered his fiancée had married his younger brother, which pretty much soured him on the idea of love and marriage. He holed up in that old farmhouse with his books and his oil paints and hardly ever came out."

"Those were his books in the auction, then," I said, thinking of the rows of World War I books at Ed Rumrill's shop.

"Yes, he was quite a military history buff. He always maintained he'd never seen any scenery in Europe that he liked any better than what he saw out his own back door. That's why he kept painting his own farm, over and over again."

I saw what he meant when I walked into the Sorrigans' living room. There was an oil painting on the wall that was a dead ringer for the one I'd found in Tom's truck this morning, except that the Sorrigans' copy had black cows and Tom's had brown and white ones. Other than that, they were identical.

"And there were several of them, you say," I said.

"Oh, yes. At least half a dozen. Here are the ones we kept out for my sisters." Charles Sorrigan pulled a couple more framed canvases out from behind a chair. "Uncle William had stipulated in his will that one of them should go to the Orange Historical Society and the rest to family members or friends who wanted them."

"There was one left over, and we put that in with the auction lot." Dorothy Sorrigan had the look of a woman who liked to get things tidied away. "We're trying to get packed up to go south tomorrow, and we had to get Uncle William's place cleaned out before then, so we could put it up for sale."

"We've just bought a place in Florida," Charlie Sorrigan added. "When I retired from the bank this year, we decided we'd had it with New England winters."

That was where I'd seen him, I thought. He'd worked at the Shawmut Bank in Orange. He just looked different in a sweater and sneakers than he had in a suit and tie.

Something else had just clicked, too. "Have you had any offers on the old farm yet?" I asked.

"No. And we don't expect to, with the real estate market the way it is right now. But the realtor is looking for tenants—in fact, she said she had a young couple very interested—so at least we'll have the rental income while we wait for the property to sell."

"Where exactly is the farm?" I asked.

"Down on Wendell Road, just past the center." For the first time it seemed to occur to Dorothy Sorrigan that I was asking a lot of rather detailed questions. "Why exactly are you so interested in Uncle William's paintings?" she asked me.

"Some young friends of mine gave me this one as a gift," I said, because it seemed simpler not to go into all the details about Tom and Jeri. "I was just curious about where it had come from, that's all."

It wasn't all, but it seemed to satisfy the Sorrigans. I thanked them and got back in the tow truck.

I drove home via Wendell Road and stopped to look at the farmhouse that had belonged to Charles Sorrigan's reclusive great uncle William. There was nothing extraordinary about the place, although the setting was pretty enough. The old white house fronted the road with a red barn out back and gently rolling fields that had once been home to the cows Uncle William had dotted so picturesquely over his paintings. There was still a faded sign on the barn door, reading "HILLVIEW FARM - Registered Aberdeen Angus."

I pulled the tow truck over and left it idling while I walked around the house. The place was clean and empty, and there didn't seem to be anything here to tell me why Tom and Jeri's painting, out of all the pictures Uncle William had done of this place, should be worth all the fuss it had caused.

I went past Haley's before going home. "Oh, yes," the proprietor said, when I showed her the painting that had been put in Tom's truck overnight. "That's the one. As I said, it's no James Franklin Gilman."

No, it was just an Uncle William, I thought. But an Uncle William that someone had apparently cared enough about to break into my lot not once but twice, enough to drug my dog and hit me on the head and cause me to do an awful lot of running around.

I felt quite sure that whoever was behind this would have been happier if I had skipped the running around part. But my curiosity was far from satisfied. My head still hurt when I leaned over too far, and I still hadn't been paid for towing Tom Wilson's truck, not to mention the business I'd lost when I'd been out of commission. All of that had built itself into an unstoppable need to know once and for all what was going on.

EIGHT

I didn't find out that Sunday afternoon, although I did manage to get a look at another one of Uncle William's paintings. I went up to the Orange Historical Society on North Main Street and was pleasantly surprised that it was open. Usually it closed earlier in the season than this, but there was a special reception going on today. An added surprise was that my old second-grade teacher was on duty as a guide. I'd known she had stayed active since her retirement. She had even founded a local program for teaching adults to read, Literacy Volunteers of Orange-Athol. But I hadn't realized she was a volunteer at the historical society, too.

It's funny—I know her first name is Barbara, but even though it's been more than forty years since I sat at a desk in her classroom, it still doesn't feel right to call her anything but Mrs. Kenney.

"You probably don't remember me, Mrs. Kenney," I said. "I'm Rita Magritte—I used to be Rita Troyanos."

"Of course I remember," she said promptly. "There was that incident with the worms."

I guess I'd hoped nobody remembered the incident with the worms but me. Schoolteachers, though, seem to have long memories. "It was an experiment," I said, a little sheepishly. "I just wanted to know whether boys were just as squeamish as girls if you dropped a worm down the back of their neck."

Barbara Kenney's eyes were sparkling in a way that made me think she knew more than I'd realized about the worm episode. "You proved it, too," she said. "I don't recall the girls being chased nearly as much for the rest of that school year."

I didn't want to go into any more detail about the worms. It hadn't been lurking feminism that had prompted me, just the same stubbornness and curiosity that had brought me to the historical society today in search of anything I could find out about Charlie Sorrigan's Uncle William.

I explained to Mrs. Kenney what I was after, and she said she recalled several boxes of old things arriving recently from

BARBARA KENNEY

an old house in Warwick. She took me upstairs to a storage room and pointed to several open crates near the door.

"I think it's all over here," she said and invited me to poke through them if I wanted. Mostly what I found were old dishes and farm implements that I guessed weren't worth very much, if none of the antique dealers at the auction had bid on them. Underneath everything else, though, there was a carefully-wrapped rectangle about the same size as the other paintings I'd seen. When I unwrapped it, I saw the now familiar white farmhouse, the red barn, the quaint groupings of black cows grazing in a green field. This canvas, like the others, was strangely muted, as though the paint had dulled over time or had been dabbed on by someone so far removed from the outside world that its colors had faded in his memory.

I examined the picture closely and even turned it over and looked on the back, but I couldn't find the answers I was looking for.

The irony was that the answer was there—at least a part of it. I just didn't realize it until early the next morning. I spent the rest of Sunday with my son Mike, making some more lasting repairs to my chain-link fence and running some barbed wire around the top of the lot for good measure. I didn't like the feeling that someone was watching my place and busting in whenever it suited him or her, and the activity put me in a grumpy mood for the calls I took that afternoon and evening.

"What's eating you?" Mike asked when I came back in from pulling a couple of kids out of a muddy spot behind the Athol Table Company building on Harrison Street.

"People who think it's fun to drive around in mud over their axles and then have to call me to get them out, among other things," I said.

"One of the other things is that loan, isn't it?" Mike asked. I had to admit it was. "I was talking to this guy at work the other day," Mike said. "He thought he might know someone who would be willing to give you a good price on on a rebuilt wrecker."

"I don't want a re-build," I said. "I want to get this business going again and do it properly or not at all. I'm tired of just scraping by. I want some reliable help with the driving, I want to be able to pay you for all the work you do on the vehicles, I want a whole day off now and then. *Drat* that telephone!"

Another call was coming in, and I knew I had to go out again. Mike was watching me sympathetically as I got my jacket back on, but he had the sense not to say anything else. Tomorrow, after I talked to my banker, I would have more to say on the subject, but tonight I was tired and frustrated by my seemingly fruitless researches about Tom Wilson's painting. Tonight I just wanted to get done with work and go to bed.

I did, and I slept well until something woke me up at seven. It might have been a sudden gust of wind in the pine trees outside or an early morning flight taking off from the airport just down the road. I don't know what it was, but my subconscious mind was still nervous, so I woke up, slid into my slippers and robe, and went out back to look.

The yard was calm enough in the clean morning light. Chili saw me at the back door and wagged his tail at the thought of an early breakfast. Everything seemed normal this morning, and after the weekend I'd had, that felt strange.

I fed the dog, made myself a cup of coffee, and sat at the table wondering what had flitted through my brain and wakened me at this hour. I let my mind wander, and after a moment, I could recall a dream I'd been having just before waking. I'd been on a farm, I remembered, wading around in muddy boots in the middle of a herd of cows. Black cows...

I sat up straight. "Aberdeen Angus cows are black," I said out loud. I'd never lived on a farm, but I knew that much about cows.

I could picture the sign on Uncle William's barn door: Hillview Farm, Registered Aberdeen Angus. And the cows in Uncle William's paintings had all been black—except for the ones in the painting that Tom and Jeri had bought. Those were brown and white—the only brown and white cows in any of the canvases I'd seen.

On the surface, that didn't answer any of my questions. But it was the first thing I'd noticed that marked Tom and Jeri's painting as unique, and I was inclined to think it might lead me to something.

The phone rang then, startling me. It was Mock's Fuel, just down the road from me. Someone had parked a motor home in front of their gate and left it locked, which meant that Mock's vehicles couldn't get out. They'd already called the police; would I come and shift the motor home a few feet?

I took the job and put my thoughts on Uncle William's brown and white cows to the back of my mind for the moment. My answering service paged me while I was out, and the day just got busier from there on.

It wasn't so busy that I forgot what was supposed to be happening today. My banker had promised to have an answer for me about my loan application, and promptly at nine o'clock I pulled over to a pay phone and called the North Quabbin Savings and Loan.

"He won't be in until one," the receptionist told me. I hung up feeling deflated.

I didn't have a chance to dwell on the delay, though. A couple of tow calls kept me busy until late in the morning, when I took time out for coffee at Woody's. There was nobody I knew at the diner today, which gave me a chance to think. Something had made Uncle William differentiate the painting Tom and Jeri had bought from all the rest of his farm pictures. Had he simply grown tired of Aberdeen Angus cattle? Had there been a period in his life when he'd farmed some other kind of cow?

I decided it was important enough to find out, if I could. I'd written the Sorrigans' phone number down yesterday when I'd talked to them. But when I called now from a pay phone at the gas station just down Main Street from the diner, there was no answer, and I remembered Dorothy Sorrigan saying they were heading to Florida today, to their new winter place.

"Drat," I said, as I hung up. How else could I find out about Uncle William?

The answer came to me almost immediately. I could look up his obituary, I thought. Uncle William had lived to be ninety-nine, and that was the kind of achievement—even for a reclusive old farmer—that people usually made a fuss over. With any luck, his obituary would tell me more about him than I knew now.

The *Athol Daily News* office was just around the corner on Exchange Street. I went in and asked about looking up the obituaries for the last few months, and was told I would need to go upstairs to the newsroom.

Upstairs, there were bound copies of the last three months' worth of newspapers. I sat down in a comfortable chair next to a window, and started going through them, sticking with the first three pages, where local news was reported.

I got all the way through the stack without finding Uncle William. I *did* notice a mention of McGarrity Brooks on one page of local news and marvelled at how the little man seemed to keep cropping up. The news item featured a picture of McGarrity looking quite pleased with himself in a bow tie. It announced that Highland Press would be publishing his forthcoming book on the tool mills of the North Quabbin region. I recalled McGarrity's fussiness with the graphic designer the other night and wondered if Highland Press was *still* publishing his book or if McGarrity's fussiness had put them off, too.

I didn't spend much time wondering about it. What I was after was Uncle William Sorrigan, and I wasn't having any luck. The Sorrigans had been very definite about the old man dying recently, I recalled. Where, then, was his obituary? Was it possible there hadn't been one printed after all?

I checked all the way back to April, switching to the microfilm machine in the next room, but I couldn't find the name Sorrigan on any of the microfilmed pages, either.

I looked at my watch; it was just after noon. I had another hour before I could call my bank again, and for the moment my beeper was quiet. I decided I had the time to double check the bound papers, in case I'd missed what I was after the first time.

I never did find William Sorrigan, for a very simple reason. There was no William Sorrigan. What I found, as I scanned the papers a second time, was an obituary for a ninety-nine-year-old Warwick farmer named William Brooks. And when I saw it, things suddenly started to fall into place.

I almost missed it, because I saw the name Brooks and thought, "There's old McGarrity again." Something made me check a little more carefully, though, and that's how I found the obit.

It didn't tell me much about Uncle William. I already knew he'd been a World War I veteran, a farmer, an amateur painter. The short column said he would be buried on August 15 and that the family had requested no flowers.

That wasn't the revealing part. It was Uncle William's last name. I had been assuming he had been a Sorrigan, but if Charlie Sorrigan's mother had been Uncle William's niece, then of course her name would have been changed by marriage. And so he wasn't a Sorrigan at all. He was a Brooks, just like McGarrity.

"You son of a gun," I said.

"Did you find the old man?" The woman at the nearest desk looked up.

"I found more than that," I said. "I found the answer."

Enough of it, anyway, to tell me where the rest of it probably was. I hurried out of the *Daily News* office and around the corner to Highland Press.

Highland Press prints stationery and business cards and posters and things—I get my invoices printed there, when I need them—and apparently, if the short article on McGarrity Brooks was any indication, they printed books, too. I decided my new idea was worth checking on, and I went in to the Highland Press office when I was done at the *Daily News*.

My beeper went off as I walked from one building to the next, and I picked up my pace a little. I didn't have a lot of time to spare, but if I was right about what was going on, there probably wasn't a lot of time to call a halt to what was going on, either. Tom and Jeri were due back from their wedding trip to Las Vegas tonight, and I wanted to fill in the rest of my blanks before they got here.

There was already a customer at Highland Press when I went in, and I waited while he talked with the man behind the counter about an estimate for printing a full-color poster. "Is this being billed to you?" the man asked.

"Yes. Reed Electronic Graphics Services. The festival is the first weekend in December, so if we can have them a month before that—"

A second employee, a woman, asked if she could help me. "It's Mrs. Henry's Towing, isn't it?" she said, and I nodded, pleased to be remembered as a customer. "Something we can reorder for you today?"

"I'm afraid not. I'm just looking for the answers to some questions, about a man named McGarrity Brooks."

I didn't expect the response I got. The two employees and the customer all looked at each other for a moment, and then they all started to laugh. "You must have been listening in on us about ten minutes ago," the customer said.

"No," I said. "Why?"

"Because we were just raking old McGarrity over the coals."

"Please," I said, "tell me more."

They were happy to. The man from Reed Electronic Graphics was apparently one of the graphic designers McGarrity had been trying to enlist for his book project, one of the many who had told him his project was unreasonable. "I mean, I've dealt with all kinds," he told me, "but I've never seen anybody so obsessed with his subject. He honestly seems to think he's going to come up with something that vast numbers of people are going to want to read. And he just doesn't understand what it will cost him to produce what's in his head."

"What would it cost, just out of interest?" I asked. "Do you have any idea?"

"Oh, I have a very good idea. When he kept telling me he wouldn't compromise on what he wanted, I finally worked up an actual price for him, just to call his bluff. To publish the book McGarrity wants would cost him at least thirty thousand, possibly more."

"I'd say more," the man behind the counter put in. "He won't be happy until he's catalogued every single tool that ever came out of north central Massachusetts—and that's a lot of tools."

"I'm assuming nobody would be paying McGarrity to publish this book," I said.

"You've got that right. It's a vanity book, all the way."

"We should be fair," the woman employee interrupted. "The poor old guy's been sick all summer. He hasn't been able to do much with that antique business of his for months. Maybe he'll finally be ready to scale down and try for a reasonable-length book."

The man from Reed Electronic Graphics looked highly skeptical. "You won't see me holding my breath waiting for *that* to happen," she said. "If anything, it'll make him more determined to publish the whole darn mess. There's already at least one very good book on the subject, but McGarrity doesn't care. He thinks this is his legacy to the world at large."

It was the word *legacy* that finally brought it all together. "Thank you," I said. "I've got to run."

I could feel their curious stares as I left the Highland Press building. There were probably more questions I could have asked them, but I had the outlines of what I needed to know, and not much time to do anything with it.

I found a pay phone and called my service, and then the wrecker and I dashed up to Winchendon and towed a station wagon back to Athol in near-record time. I made another call to my bank when I was done and was told that my loan officer was in a meeting for another half hour. I refrained from saying exactly what I thought about that and was trying to figure out whether I had time to get to McGarrity Brooks' house and back before the bank closed at three, when my beeper went off again.

The towing call took longer than it should have, because the guy who'd called me had run his new car off a narrow road north of Orange in a place where there was virtually no way for me to get at it. "You did this on purpose, right?" I muttered, as I angled the wrecker back and forth. I finally got the car back up the embankment, but its right front bumper was so crumpled that it interfered with the wheel, and I ended up towing it all the way to Newcomb Motors on Daniel Shays Highway in Athol. By the time I'd done that it was after three o'clock, and I had missed my chance to talk to my banker today.

"Oh, hell," I said, looking at my watch. I was going to have to wait another day to find out about my loan.

I knew it wasn't all the fault of Tom and Jeri's painting. But at the moment all my frustrations seemed to fasten on that and on the time and money I'd lost this weekend tracking down clues to a mystery that wasn't even mine.

"That does it," I said, climbing back into the cab of my truck. "I am going to sort this thing out once and for all." It wasn't just the bump on my head, or the money that the break-in on my lot was going to cost me, or the delay about the loan. I just don't like being lied to, and someone had lied to me in a major way over the past few days. I put the wrecker in gear and headed it north.

NINE

There was no car in McGarrity Brooks' driveway. That alone should have tipped me off, I thought. The first time I'd been here, there had been no car either. The second time, the car belonging to the woman from Spaulding Graphics had been here, but it had been alone. Nobody lived on an isolated road like this without a vehicle of some sort. Where had McGarrity's car been all weekend? It hadn't occurred to me to wonder before.

I knew now, of course. And that made me even madder. I wasn't the only one who'd been lied to, the only one who'd been cheated.

I knocked firmly on the door but didn't get an answer. I knocked again, waited, and then decided to try McGarrity's shop out back.

The piece of plywood was still nailed over the window that had been broken, but I could see light showing around the edges of the garage doors. It was starting to get dark already; the sky was cloudy, and there was the feel of impending winter in the air.

I was steamed up enough that I didn't feel the cold. "McGarrity?" I said loudly, rapping on the wooden doors. "Are you in there?"

His neatly combed head appeared in the door a moment later. "Well, hello, Mrs. Magritte," he said, sounding surprised. "I didn't expect—"

"No, I don't imagine you did." I went into the shop, not waiting to be invited. "You expected I would buy your story about your shop being broken into. You thought I would imagine you had nothing to do with Tom Wilson's painting being stolen, didn't you?"

He frowned at me. "Really, Mrs. Magritte," he said. "The shop *was* broken into. You can still see some of the broken glass, there, in the corner." He pointed to show me the place.

I turned to look, because the astonishment in his voice sounded so real that I suddenly wondered if I'd been wrong after all. What happened next proved that I wasn't.

As I shifted my gaze, two things happened. One was that the lights went out. And as they did, something hooked me around my ankles, so I lost my balance and fell to the hard concrete floor I suddenly couldn't see. There was a brief flash of light as McGarrity opened the door, and then it shut again, leaving me in darkness.

The lump on my skull had started feeling better in the last day or two. But the shock of the unexpected fall made my head spin again, and it was a few seconds before I could clamber back to my feet. By the time I'd done that, a series of noises outside told me McGarrity was making sure that I would stay locked up for some time to come.

"I'm sorry to have to do this," I could hear him saying quite clearly over the sound of scraping and banging. "But my timetable is rather tight, and I really can't have you barging around in the middle of things right now."

I couldn't see a damn thing, but that didn't stop me from feeling my way around the edge of the shop, knocking things onto the floor as I went, and pounding on the garage doors from the inside.

"You're wasting your time," McGarrity told me. "They're fastened from the outside, plus I've got a piece of two-by-four through the handles. And in a minute you're going to be even more securely locked up."

I heard the slam of a very familiar door. He was getting into the cab of my truck, I realized. I felt in my pocket, momentarily reassured by the presence of my key ring, and then I realized he wouldn't need the keys.

McGarrity's driveway sloped down to the garage at a slight angle. All he needed to do was put the wrecker in neutral and let it coast slowly down until it was touching the garage doors, and I would be neatly imprisoned by my own truck.

A gentle bump against the doors a moment later told me that was exactly what he'd done. The door slammed, and I heard McGarrity say, "Such a fitting accident, really. When I get back, I'll call the police to tell them you seemed to have come back to break into my shop a second time—"

"Wait a minute," I said. "I didn't break in the first time!"

"The police won't know that. I'll tell them you must have left the truck in neutral, and it rolled against the doors, keeping you in there until I got back and called them." I heard the lock being turned now and the two-by-four being withdrawn. There would be no proof that McGarrity had locked me in here himself and plenty of circumstantial evidence to support the story he was planning to tell the police.

I was getting madder and madder, thinking about it. "Don't you dare leave me here!" I shouted at him. "After everything you've done—" I stopped in mid blast, as what he'd said got through to me. "What do you mean, when you get back?" I demanded. "Where are you going?"

The sound of a car engine closer to the road interrupted me. "Really," McGarrity said, "you didn't leave me much time to spare. Don't bother yelling, please. We won't hear you from the house."

It must be Tom and Jeri, I realized, back from Las Vegas. They would be driving McGarrity's car, and they would be completely in the dark about what had been going on.

So far McGarrity hadn't done anything worse than break into my lot and knock me out. But if my guesses were right, he was getting close to laying his hands on what might be a very great deal of money, money he wanted desperately for a project he'd been dreaming about for years. What might he do, if something stood in the way of that?

Would he be capable of hurting the young couple who were even now returning the car he must have lent them on Thursday night? I didn't know. I only knew that I couldn't just sit here in the darkened shop and let McGarrity Brooks get away with what I thought he was trying to do.

My head was aching again, but I managed to scramble around and find the light-switch on the wall. I would have been more than willing to break the window, except that it was covered with plywood. I was going to have to find some other way out, and fast. McGarrity would be talking to Tom and Jeri up at the house, telling them he was sorry he hadn't been able to look at their painting because Tom's truck had been towed before he could get to it. He'd be happy to drive them home, since they wouldn't be able to get the truck back until tomorrow. And then they'd be gone, and I would have lost my only chance to prove that McGarrity was trying to swindle the young couple out of the future they'd bought fair and square.

The walls of the garage looked annoyingly well-built. And I knew there was no hope of trying to shift the wrecker from in front of the doors. The place was full of tools, though. I ought to be able to think of *something*...

I took a closer look at the plywood over the window. Anybody else would have just banged in a few nails and called someone to repair it, I thought. But not McGarrity Brooks. Having smashed his own window to make it look like a break-in, he had proceeded to screw a piece of plywood over the open hole with the same obsessive precision he brought to everything else he did.

"Gotcha," I said, as I picked up a screwdriver from the workbench.

Getting the plywood off was the easy part. I pulled a chair over to the door and stood on it, but even so, it was a real job to get my shoulders out the window. And then there were my hips, about which the less said, the better. I ended up falling palms down on the hood of the wrecker, cursing the too-small window and my own ample figure and McGarrity Brooks. I hoped like hell nobody was watching, for dignity's sake as well as secrecy's.

I wasn't any too soon getting free of the garage. I could hear the car engine starting up again, and I got into the wrecker as fast as I could. It was darker now, but I didn't put the headlights on. I didn't want McGarrity to know I was after him if I could avoid it.

His taillights were easy enough to follow at first. "If I had a new truck with a radio in it," I said out loud, "I could be calling the cops right now."

But I didn't have a radio; I didn't even have a bank loan, yet. And I was having an increasingly hard time seeing the road, as we drove into heavier forest where the trees overhung the road on both sides.

After I'd hit two bad potholes in a row, I realized I was going to have to turn my lights on or risk hitting something in the dark. Was it my imagination, or did McGarrity start to pick up speed as soon as I'd done it? I went a little faster, too, and this time there was no doubt about it. The man didn't want anybody on his tail, even though he probably didn't know yet that it was me.

He was going faster all the time, and I was starting to worry seriously about losing him. Aside from its asthma problems, the old wrecker never had been a vehicle for high-speed chases, and if McGarrity really bolted, there was no way I could keep up. "It's now or never, old girl," I said to the truck, and I turned all my flashing lights on full blast.

I saw a young woman's startled face in the back window of McGarrity's car. He wouldn't be expecting the tow truck, I kept telling myself. He would think I was a cop, and if he expected to keep up his innocent citizen act, he would be smart to pull over and play dumb.

He didn't, though. He must have been more panicked than I realized, because his car just kept picking up speed. "Hell," I said. Was I going to lose him after all?

And then, without warning, I did lose him—completely and utterly, and so suddenly that for a moment I thought I was seeing things. Or rather, *not* seeing things, because one moment McGarrity's red taillights were there ahead of me on the road, and the next moment they simply weren't.

I'd hurtled along for nearly half a mile before I realized he'd vanished. I tromped on the brakes and heard my own tires squeal against the pavement. "Son of a gun," I said. "Where did you go?"

It only took me a moment to figure it out. There was an old road leading off into the woods just about where McGarrity had disappeared. There was a gravel pit at the end of it, and the reason I knew it was there was that I had pulled somebody's car out of it one summer a couple of years ago. McGarrity lived just up the road; he must know the gravel pit, too.

I did a screeching four-point turn and drove back to the spot. It wasn't easy to see, with the darkness descending all around and the trees reaching their branches out of the dimness like unfriendly arms. For a moment I thought I'd missed the old road, but then I heard a car door slam, off to my right, and I knew I was close.

Other drivers think about getting *into* places: tow truck drivers think about how they're going to get *out* again. It's second nature. I had a vague idea about grabbing up Tom and Jeri if I could, and high-tailing it out of here, which is why, when I found the wooded road, I backed my way along it, engine whining in protest. I wanted to be able to make a quick exit if I needed to.

The gravel pit road was disused and bumpy, and I got jostled around in the seat, but my mind was focused on those two kids up there. They would know for sure that something was up now, if they hadn't suspected it before, and McGarrity was going to have a tough time explaining why he'd taken off into the woods like this.

I shut off the engine but stayed in the truck. When I had rolled my window down, I could just barely hear McGarrity's voice saying crossly, "Just shut up. Don't say a thing."

"Hey, I guess we can talk if we want to." It was the young man's voice, puzzled and angry. He had barely gotten the words out when the loud crack of a gunshot echoed through the trees, followed by at least one frightened gasp.

"Shut *up*!" McGarrity repeated, more edgily now.

Great, I thought. I had known, in the back of my imagination, that this might happen, that he might be desperate enough to be carrying a weapon. It didn't change my plans, but it did make it more important to get things right.

Into the long silence that followed the gunshot, Tom Wilson spoke again, more cautiously this time. "Who's that chasing you?" he asked.

"It's a very long story."

"Sure it is." I spoke loudly, to make sure all three of them heard me. "Did he tell you the part yet about how he stole something that was hidden behind the painting you bought at Haley's?"

The whole forest seemed momentarily hushed, taking in what I'd said. Then McGarrity said irritably, "That's ridiculous."

"It's the only explanation that makes sense," I said. "Why else would someone break into Tom's truck on my lot, steal the painting, and then break in again to put the painting back?"

There was another pause. "Why *would* someone do that?" Tom Wilson asked finally.

"Because there was something about this painting that he knew was worth a lot of money. Once he'd gotten you two safely out of town for the long weekend, he figured he had the painting to himself—to remove whatever was hidden behind it, and then to 'value' as a worthless landscape. Unfortunately, your truck got towed before he could do that, so he had to change his plans."

"Is this true?" a woman's voice asked. "Who are you, anyway?"

"I'm the tow truck driver Tom called on Thursday night," I said. "I towed your truck before McGarrity could get to the painting that was under the seat, and he spent the rest of the weekend trying to get it without anyone knowing about it. I still don't know exactly what made him so desperate, but I'm willing to bet that whatever he took is in his car at this moment. In fact—"

A startled squawk from McGarrity made me think I must be right, and I plunged on. "In fact, my guess is he's planning to drop you off and then head straight for Boston or New York or somewhere else where he can unload his prize and turn it into money that should by rights belong to the two of you. The evidence will be gone, and he'll be a rich man. Am I right, McGarrity?"

"You're out of your mind," McGarrity said. "She's been hounding me. It has nothing to do with you two."

"Then how does she know about our painting?" Jeri demanded.

"Yeah," Tom put in. "I *wondered* why you were so willing to rent us your car last week. You seemed pretty eager to help out a couple of strangers."

"Nice touch, McGarrity," I said. "Renting them your car, I mean. Make a little more money out of them."

"I was just trying to be practical," McGarrity said. "After all, they had a plane to catch. I just wanted—"

"Spare me the baloney," I said. "You wanted whatever your Uncle William had hidden behind that painting. He told you it was there, didn't he? The two sides of the family were estranged, because your father had stolen away the girl Uncle William loved. But he must have had a soft spot for you somewhere. He told you the painting with the brown and white cows in it had a secret that would make you rich after he died. Isn't that right?"

"Wow," Jeri said.

"And you wanted the money, so you could finance that book of yours before *you* died. With enough money, you could make the designers and photographers and printers do exactly what you wanted."

I had more to say, but I never got to it. Another shot boomed through the woods, and McGarrity's words came while the reverberation was still dying away.

"Be quiet!" His voice was shrill now. He sounded hysterical, which I didn't think was a very good combination with the gun. "All of you, be quiet! I *was* going to let you go. This was going to be *her* fault—the woman with the tow truck. And the young people wouldn't have known or cared about the painting. They just liked the farm scene, just like Uncle William. That was all he cared about, his farm and his cows. That was why he stole the sketch. He said it reminded him of home. And it was wartime—all kinds of things happened and nobody thought twice about it. The art gallery had already been looted—nobody else wanted the picture, because it was just pen and ink. It's just that it looked like Uncle William's farm, and it happened to be by Van Gogh—"

He stopped suddenly, as if he hadn't meant to say this much. Now that he had, I realized, all three of us knew far more than he could let us get away with, if he wanted to turn Uncle William's purloined Van Gogh sketch into the fortune he'd been counting on.

I squinted in the growing darkness and could just make out McGarrity holding a pistol at arm's length, bracing one arm with the other. Unfortunately, he looked as though he knew what to do with the weapon. On the other hand, he didn't seem to be carrying a sketch by Van Gogh, or anybody else. That was probably still in the car, I realized.

As quietly as I could, I got out of the wrecker. I still spoke loudly, to cover up what I was doing. "You could share it with them," I said. "They bought the painting, after all. They're legally entitled to the proceeds."

This was greeted with stony silence. The clanking as I pushed the lever in the bed of the truck was suddenly loud in the forest, and McGarrity said testily, "What are you doing?"

"Giving these kids another chance," I said. "Tom, Jeri, listen to me. Can you see McGarrity's face?"

"Yeah. Sort of." Tom sounded nervous. I didn't blame him.

"Good. If he turns away—if he turns to look at me—you two take off, all right?"

"Are you trying to get us killed?" Jeri demanded. "He's got a gun."

"Right. But it's only one gun, and there are three of us. He can't kill us all at once. Just do what I'm telling you."

Another shot sang out, and I heard the bullet whistle through the woods to my right. I kept working, lowering the cradle, pulling down the hook. I kept my head down, too.

"I *will* kill them," McGarrity said, "if you don't stop."

"Then I'll tow your precious sketch right to the police station, and you'll lose everything you've waited for all these years," I said, as evenly as I could. I hated putting the two kids in this position, but I didn't see a better way out. "You'd be better off trying to shoot me, McGarrity. That way, you'll still have your sketch. You can take off to Tahiti or somewhere on the proceeds and live the rest of your life in luxury. Of course, you'll have to buy yourself a new passport, and there probably isn't much of a market in Tahiti for books on the tool mills of north central Massachusetts, but—"

My speech ran out at just about the same time as McGarrity's patience. I heard him snarl as he started toward me through the carpet of fallen leaves, but by then I had finished hooking up his car and was heading for the driver's seat. "Run!" I yelled at Tom and Jeri and flung myself into the cab.

The wrecker wheezed—sputtered—nearly started—coughed again. By the time the engine finally turned over, I had promised it green pastures for the rest of its days if it would only get me out of here now. By then, too, McGarrity Brooks had loosed off another round in my direction.

The first one missed, but the second one went through the passenger window and out the windshield. It was one of those odd moments where you simply do what you've decided to do and put fear on hold. I saw the windshield shatter and felt the safety glass falling in on me like sudden hail, but I concentrated on driving and getting out of there with McGarrity's car and his priceless Van Gogh sketch.

We did it, the wrecker and I. I heard another shot and wondered how many he had left. By then I was nearly to the main road, with the car bumping along behind me. If I could just stay ahead of that next shot—

I found out later that he never got to fire it. His heart shuddered under the strain of fear and fury and exertion, and he didn't even make it as far as the road. While I was frantically heading for the nearest house and the nearest telephone, Tom and Jeri were crashing through the darkened forest looking for help. And McGarrity Brooks was lying in a bed of fallen leaves, trying to get his breath and probably, judging by the little I knew of the man, saying some very unfriendly things about his late Uncle William.

EPILOGUE

"But how did you know what was hidden behind the painting with the cows?" my daughter Hannah wanted to know.

"I didn't." I smoothed my skirt over my knees. I hate wearing skirts and do it as little as possible, but the occasion seemed to call for it. "I just knew it had to be something valuable, if somebody was willing to break into my lot and risk killing me for it. And when they broke in again and put the painting back, it could only mean that whatever was valuable about the painting wasn't there any more."

"So the sketch was sandwiched between two layers of canvas," Mike said. He and Hannah were sitting on either side of me in the North Quabbin Savings and Loan's waiting area.

"Right. Old Uncle William knew he had something worth hiding, all right. He'd picked it out of a looted art gallery in a French town during the war, not for mercenary reasons, but simply because it reminded him of his farm back home."

It did, too. I'd seen the little Van Gogh sketch when the police had searched McGarrity's car. It was a beautiful thing, done, the art expert had told us, during the happiest period of Van Gogh's unhappy life, and somehow managing to convey an unmistakable sense of contentment and peace. No wonder Uncle William Brooks had wanted it in the middle of a war.

"When Uncle William got home, he tried to find out whether it was worth anything and was told it might be worth a stiff prison sentence, if he couldn't prove he'd come by it honestly," I went on. "He hid it away then, because he loved the sketch and didn't want to be accused of stealing it. And he told his young nephew, McGarrity, that the painting with the brown and white cows would be McGarrity's after Uncle William had died, and it would make his fortune for him."

"So McGarrity didn't know what was behind the painting?" Mike said.

"No. Not until he'd stolen it out of Tom and Jeri's truck."

"How did he know it was in Tom and Jeri's truck?" Hannah demanded.

"McGarrity had been sick all summer, recovering from heart trouble. He'd been out of commission when Uncle William died, and when his effects were being auctioned off. Everyone else in the family had been around to claim their picture of the old farm, but McGarrity had missed his. And so it got into the auction and then into Haley's barn. By the time he was on his feet again, it had been sold to Tom Wilson and Jeri Crozier."

"Who were hoping to rent the house," Hannah put in.

"Yes. They finally had enough money to afford a place of their own, and enough—after Jeri won that lottery ticket—to fly to Vegas and get married, away from her jealous ex-boyfriend and her two brothers, who didn't want her to have anything to do with Tom. Jeri told me she fell in love with the painting as soon as she saw it and decided they had to splurge and buy it. She thought it would bring them good luck. And it seemed that it had, when they saw an ad in the paper saying that anyone with pastoral landscapes of New England—especially with cows in them—should have them valued, because they could be worth thousands of dollars."

"McGarrity put the ad in, right?" Mike said.

"Right. And when Tom and Jeri called, he got them all fired up about the idea that they had a James Franklin Gilman or something else rare and valuable. He was going to convince them to leave it with him for the weekend, which would give him a chance to get whatever Uncle William had hidden. But they slid off the road in the storm and robbed him of the opportunity."

"Enter Henry's Towing," Mike grinned. "And a tow truck driver too stubborn to keep her nose out of other people's business."

"It *was* my business," I insisted. "Tom Wilson owed me for that tow."

"Well, he'll be able to pay you now," Hannah said. "And then some."

There was already an artistic and legal uproar going on over the Van Gogh sketch that was making a noise far beyond our corner of the state. But it looked as though Tom and Jeri would be entitled to the proceeds of the eventual sale of the sketch, and that it would set them up in a style that would make their dreams of buying and fixing up the old Warwick farmhouse seem like small potatoes.

"You know," Hannah said, with that overtone of disapproval in her voice, "if McGarrity Brooks just presented his case to them honestly, he probably could have talked them into splitting the money with him. They seem like a very reasonable couple."

"I know," I said, "but McGarrity Brooks is a man who feels society doesn't appreciate him as much as it should. He wasn't going to share his prize with anybody."

We'd been waiting for fifteen minutes in the bank, because I'd finally arranged an appointment to talk to my loan officer. Mike and Hannah had taken time off to come with me—for moral support, they said. I had a suspicion they'd been talking about me between themselves and come to the conclusion that maybe it wasn't quite safe for their mother to be running around loose on her own.

My banker put his head around the corner at last, and Mike and Hannah stood up when I did. This was it, I thought: the moment when the fate of Henry's Towing would be decided. I had felt far less nervous confronting McGarrity Brooks and his pistol in the woods last night.

"Rita." The loan officer smiled at me. "We've just been discussing your adventures. Come in, all of you."

My adventures of the past week were hardly likely to recommend me to a banker as a pillar of reliability and fiscal responsibility, I thought. My knees were slightly shaky as I went into the small office and sat down.

"You know that we have to follow fairly strict guidelines when we assess the stability of a business," my banker said.

I could kiss the loan goodbye, I thought. The whole affair with McGarrity Brooks and the stolen Van Gogh sketch was going to pull the plug on my chances of building up the towing company. I'd never realized until that moment just how much I loved my job, and how much I wanted to keep it.

"I've been reading all about you in the *Daily News* these last few days," the loan officer went on, "and I must say I hadn't realized you were such a risk taker, Rita."

Banks don't like risks. I knew that. They like predictability, order, all those things I had failed to display this past few days.

"We've always thought of Henry's as a fairly small, unambitious venture. That's why we've been so careful in going over your plans for expansion."

Great, I thought. I'd proved Henry's Towing was a harebrained, fly-by-night organization, and that meant there wasn't going to be any expansion, or any Henry's Towing, for that matter.

"But after this weekend—"

I fought back the urge to sigh.

"After this weekend, we're convinced that you have the motivation to handle much more than you've been doing to date. So we're approving the loan request in full. I've got the check here. Frankly, Rita—" I heard the amusement in his voice before I'd really taken in what the words meant. "Frankly, if you could track down a missing masterpiece and handle nearly every tow call that came in at the same time, we don't have any doubt that you'll be able to do everything you say you're planning on. Congratulations."

Mike made a noise more appropriate for a football field than a bank office, but the banker didn't seem to mind. Hannah was hugging me, and somebody else was shaking my hand. I was too dazed to realize exactly what had just happened, much less to follow the conversation, which was drifting rapidly into talk of costs and projections and new vehicles and hiring procedures.

"Excuse me," I said. "I'll be right back, but first I have to go break the good news to someone who's been waiting to hear it."

I escaped to the parking lot where the old wrecker was parked. "I did it," I said out loud, leaning against the hood. I didn't know if I was talking to the truck or to Henry's memory or to myself, or just to the clear October air. "I really did it. We're not going under, after all."

It was more than just not going under, and I knew it. I'd been following my instincts ever since I'd gotten that first call from Tom Wilson, and in spite of some severe misgivings along the way, those instincts had landed me, at last, exactly where I had wanted to be. It was a vindication I hadn't even been looking for, but all the more welcome because of that.

"You'd have been proud of me, Henry," I said, because I suddenly found myself missing him. "I learned some things this weekend."

In the future, I thought, I was going to have to charge extra to customers who ended up with fabulously valuable pieces of artwork as a result of my efforts.

In the future I was going to treat myself to a day off every week or so, because although I wasn't showing any rust and I didn't wheeze going up hills yet, I was just as middle-aged as the wrecker was, and the past weekend had made me realize that a little maintenance wasn't such a bad idea for me, too. In fact, I was planning to begin with a week off before started working on the new, improved Henry's Towing.

And once I got back to work again, I promised myself, I was going to think long and hard before the next time I towed an empty vehicle on a dark and stormy night.

LITERACY VOLUNTEERS OF ORANGE-ATHOL

Literacy Volunteers of Orange-Athol provides free, confidential, one-to-one tutoring for adults who want help with reading, writing, or learning English as a second language. The program is affiliated with Literacy Volunteers of America, a leading advocate for improved adult literacy for more than thirty years.

TROUBLE IN TOW has been made possible through Cathy Stanton's creativity and the contributors whose names appear in the story. These individuals and businesses have a commitment to improving literacy in our community. Thanks to them, all proceeds from the sale of this book will go directly to supporting Literacy Volunteers' tutoring activities.

For more information about Literacy Volunteers, contact their office in the Athol Memorial Building.

LITERACY VOLUNTEERS OF ORANGE-ATHOL
584 Main Street
Athol, Massachusetts   01331

508.249.5381